# THE BIG RIVER

PETER RIMMER

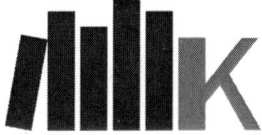

# ABOUT PETER RIMMER

Peter Rimmer was born in London, England, and grew up in the south of the city where he went to school. After the Second World War, aged eighteen, he joined the Royal Air Force, reaching the rank of Pilot Officer before he was nineteen. At the end of his National Service, he sailed for Africa to grow tobacco in what was then Rhodesia, now Zimbabwe.

The years went by and Peter found himself in Johannesburg where he established an insurance brokering company. Over 2% of the companies listed on the Johannesburg Stock Exchange were clients of Rimmer Associates. He opened branches in the United States of America, Australia and Hong Kong and travelled extensively between them.

Having lived a reclusive life on his beloved smallholding in Knysna, South Africa, for over 25 years, Peter passed away in July 2018. He has left an enormous legacy of unpublished work for his family to release over the coming years, and not only they but also his readers from around the world will sorely miss him. Peter Rimmer was 81 years old.

To read more about Peter's life, please visit his website: https://www.peterrimmer.com/novelist/author/

# ALSO BY PETER RIMMER

**The Brigandshaw Chronicles**
*The Rise and Fall of the Anglo Saxon Empire*
Book 1 - Echoes from the Past
Book 2 - Elephant Walk
Book 3 - Mad Dogs and Englishmen
Book 4 - To the Manor Born
Book 5 - On the Brink of Tears
Book 6 - Treason If You Lose
Book 7 - Horns of Dilemma
Book 8 - Lady Come Home
Book 9 - The Best of Times
Book 10 - Full Circle
Book 11 - Leopards Never Change Their Spots
Book 12 - Look Before You Leap
Book 13 - The Game of Life
Book 14 - Scattered to the Wind
Book 15 - When Friends Become Lovers

**Standalone Novels**
All Our Yesterdays
Cry of the Fish Eagle
Just the Memory of Love
Vultures in the Wind
In the Beginning of the Night
The Big River

**The Asian Sagas**
Bend with the Wind (Book 1)
Each to His Own (Book 2)

**The Pioneers**
Morgandale (Book 1)
Carregan's Catch (Book 2)

**Novella**
Second Beach

THE BIG RIVER

Copyright © Peter Rimmer 2023

This novel is entirely a work of fiction. Names, characters, long-standing establishments, places, events and incidents are either the products of the author's imagination or used in a fictitious manner. Any resemblance to actual persons, living or dead, is purely coincidental.

First published in Great Britain in April 2023 by

KAMBA PUBLISHING, United Kingdom

10 9 8 7 6 5 4 3 2 1

Peter Rimmer asserts the moral right to be identified as the author of this work.

All rights reserved. No part of this publication may be reproduced or transmitted in any form or by any means, electronic or mechanical, including photocopy, recording, or any information storage and retrieval system, without permission in writing from Kamba Publishing at books@peterrimmer.com.

# FOREWORD

∼

When we, at Kamba Publishing, first began working with *The Big River* manuscript, we had an intriguing task to uncover. We weren't exactly sure what time it was set in, nor when it was written. Unlike the *Brigandshaw* series, which had clear timestamps for each book, there was no indication given for *The Big River*. To solve this mystery, we had to sift through Peter's private papers. In the 60s and the following decades, it was not easy for writers to get published, but Peter was persistent in sending out many letters, only to receive rejections.

In amongst his papers, we found a letter from an agent dated July 1965, expressing interest in receiving a copy of *The Big River*. There was our answer. Probably written in 1965 or thereabouts. But tantalising there is a reference in the book to the country Tanganyika which was renamed Tanzania in April 1964. Was this a slip of Peter's memory or could it have been written pre-April 1964? Something we'll never know. Regardless, we decided the story should begin in 1964, changing Tanganyika to Tanzania.

Also to note, in the early 60s, Peter was at the beginning of his writing career, experimenting with different writing styles, and *The Big River* is the first that we have published written in the first person, unlike his later books.

We hope you enjoy *The Big River* as much as we have, and welcome your thoughts on social media, or please do write a review, links to which are provided at the end of the book.

Thank you.

Heather Stretch, Kamba Publishing

# PART ONE

1963

# 1

*I* came out here for Kariba ten years ago. I was employed on the dynamos that now generate the country's electricity. The Italian contractors were short of engineers. For them it was enough that I could do the job and degrees didn't matter so much. I didn't want to do electrical engineering then any more than I do now.

I haven't achieved anything except a divorce and that wasn't difficult before or after. I don't know why I married Elio any more than I know why I came to Rhodesia. For nothing better to do? Well, what better than sitting here and drinking a cold beer? The fan whirrs in front of me on the mantelpiece and faces itself in turn to all parts of the sparse room that has doors into the kitchen, bedrooms and veranda. There are three chairs in the small room and skins on the floor and badly made curtains over the gauzed windows.

I think of Stella Marsham, though maybe I shouldn't. She was married three months ago but the honeymoon in Europe will have been different to her new life among the sugar. Her husband did the same as me by going home and appearing rich and thinking how nice it would be not to look at the girlie magazines at the start of the hot nights.

I drink and put down the empty beer glass and go outside by pushing the gauze screen. Out here is the hot sweat of an African night. I smell the river. I scratch inside my shirt at yesterday's tsetse bites with satisfaction. There isn't any fat on the five foot ten of me. Not bad at thirty-four. The hard bristles on my chin need shaving. Over there is the club. Light floods up from it into the trees.

I walk down the veranda steps onto the harsh grass of the lawn and on into the moon-made shadows of trees that overhang the driveway.

I get into the open Land Rover, start the engine – gear, clutch, and I move forward into the night. I turn, parallel with the club, and accelerate. The silhouettes of night draw me towards the river. The cane goes by on both sides in a silent black line against the night. There's a huge full moon up there.

THE SMOOTH SHEET of the river moves under the moon. The sand is wet between my toes. Fixed into the river sand, I seem to have a meaning. The gnarled black claws of the trees grasp up for anything on either side of me. I watch and feel for movement. A hippo grunts. I look up at the night sky and then at the dark, motionless bush and down further at the moon's reflection on the water and shiver in the heat.

I turn and walk back and my feet are heavy, sunk down in the wet sand. Hoof marks are deep in the fine grains of water-and-wind-smoothed silica. The need is to drink and stay alive. Feet-shaped prints and hoof-shaped prints. It doesn't tell the colour of the feet. Here there is only natural destruction. The moon hides little. It creates the shadow and unsoftens the night. Ten years I've been here. Those ten can't be destroyed like Stella's marriage, like mine. She has the power to make me think of her.

A dugout glides on the far side of the water. A leopard coughs and is answered – a lone cough, lonely, from the Zambian shore, the silent, black shore of black Africa. Treated right, the river is friendly to both sides.

I walk up the steep bank with roots of sand-grass under my feet. The sinews in my right hand tense. I pull the 8mm off my shoulder. My fingers clutch at the point of balance. Buffalo and elephant make noise and this is too big for the small buck. I widen my eyes to look harder into the darkness. My left hand moves towards the searchlight switch at my hip. Wait! Now! The eyes flash as it claws at nothing and sinks. I smash another shell into the breach and fire. The new sand is cold under my feet. A dead, female leopard. The bullet has smashed her nose and penetrated the length of her body. The other hole is an inch to the right. I get the tail over my shoulder and pull. The carcase grovels its way behind me.

I drop her length beside the Land Rover and wedge the rifle in the bracket along the inside of the windscreen. I turn back and bend down and pick up the tail, pull her round and heave the animal over the tailboard. I have no licence for leopard so I will skin her tonight and nail it under the roof in the attic. Leopards normally leap faster than that. She must have thought like a human for that second before death. I get into the driver's seat.

The car's headlights rush out and over the river and lose themselves in the small trees and rising banks of Zambia. Kwacha! Freedom for the people, purchased by the new life. The buffalo will die quicker for the people's freedom. From everything to nothing in eighty years! The engine sends the sound of new life out over the river in pursuit of the shadows. I reverse and the beam turns and juts down to the surface with the moon on the river. Now it sweeps on into Rhodesia. Into first gear and we bump forward and I push down for power.

She will be in the club. It will make a diversion. Without a need for this I would be free to drive contentedly along this wheel-rutted track. Do I want to get in among the lights at the club? No, I'll go home with the dead leopard and think about myself being the one who's alive. Oh, what the hell does it matter? I'll gain nothing but a moral righteousness. There's no reason for keeping away. She can be my purpose for the moment. The women here are either married or don't exist so I haven't any choice. It isn't wrong out here. Her husband, Jim, did the same as me before he brought her back. Maybe he'll change back to his old habits.

A MFUTI TREE leans down from high over the one-storey club and catches up the light in its wood and patches of leaves. I circle the wheel and the Land Rover bumps in at the club turning. The leopard lurches and smacks dully against the metal floor behind me. I brake and slew round onto the gravelled space in front of the club. The light from the windows seeps as far as it's able to penetrate the night. I stop beside a msasa tree. I turn out the lights and the Land Rover is pressed into the darkness. I cut the engine. The sound of white Africa comes in. The noise of recorded band music rises above the gaggle of voices, laughter and a scream of delight. I put on my shoes by feel and open the low door, get out and crunch the gravel with my leather soles and walk towards their laughter. I flex the index finger that pulled the trigger and scratch its joint.

# 2

"Guido! Come and have a drink. We've been waiting for you to give some life to this place."

"Thanks, Jim. I'd like a cold Castle. It's hot outside. I went down to the river to cool off."

"Did you shoot anything? Hey, Ted, fancy you being here tonight. Guido's been down to the river. Go and have a look in the back of his truck. You'll get a raise from the Game Department for catching Guido Martelli poaching. Your beer, you poaching bastard."

"I wouldn't bring a carcase back to the club, now would I? Cheers to you all – Stella, Jim and you too, Ted. Yes, that's nice for my stomach. I shall have to drink quickly. I can see I've a lot to catch up on."

"What do you do at the river at this time of night?"

"Why are women so practical? I went down to look at the moon on the water and think of you, Stella."

"And what did you kill down there while you were thinking?"

"A leopard, Ted, that'll measure all of six feet."

"They don't come that big around here."

"No, I didn't think so either. Mzenga, give us another round and put it on my card."

She is wearing a thin cotton dress that has large blue dragons on the white background – that and sandals. Her breasts push firmly into the soft material. The bra underneath must be smooth as it doesn't make a pattern through the cloth. Her skin matches the smoothness. She isn't tall but her legs are in proportion to the rest of her body and her calves are hard with the pressure from her high heels. The flesh on her arms and body is thick and firm.

I concentrate on the drinks and get myself out of the repartee. It's mostly like this in the club, except there isn't usually a woman to alleviate my boredom. She has a lot of sex, this woman. I wonder if she is conscious of what I would like to do to her. Strange the game warden being in the club tonight. I haven't seen him for weeks.

"Here's your drink, Stella."

She smiles appreciatively and wrinkles her nose at me. Very pert! The game warden taps me on the shoulder. He is long and thin and gaunt. Officially he doesn't like me.

"Well, I must be getting along. You don't mind if I look in the back of your Land Rover, Guido? I have to substantiate my working hours in reports to Salisbury."

"Help yourself. It looks to me just over six feet."

"If you say that too often I'll believe you! Thanks for the drink."

Well, what does it matter? He can confiscate my best gun and fine me fifty pounds. It will make him happy and in that way the killing will have created something. There is so much noise in here. How much false conversation does one make in a lifetime! As we drink we talk louder. The overhead fans make no impression on the tired, airless atmosphere. I lean back against the wooden bar and drink outside the conversation. One exchange of definite feeling with her is more valuable than two. I count people in bars. There are eighteen tonight. I know them all except the two talking to the managing director – that's Max Rosher. He's smooth. At forty the muscle around his shoulders and stomach is still hard. Around the high part of the bar's walls, black and white murals of monkeys and buck and buffalo smile down on us. Outside, someone is swimming in the fierce blaze of the arc lights. Looking through the French windows with my elbows on the bar I can't see who it is. The gram's playing arm swings away and another record thumps down on top of the last. This is the record that has been favourite for six months.

"You look as though you're going to sleep."

I smile. He half returns the gesture before looking back into his beer glass. With just a little more fat on his hulk, Jim will change from debonair to gross.

She touches her husband's arm to get his attention.

"Why don't we swim? There's someone in the pool already. It looks cool. My costume is still in the changing room. Come on, Guido, it will wake you up. Drink down that beer and have another quickly. You'll feel more like a party. We mustn't let the visiting shareholders think we don't use the pool they provided."

"You mean the two over there?"

"Yes, Jim told me who they were."

"Do you know what they're doing here, Guido?"

"No... No, I don't."

"Pity. I thought they might have told you.

"They can't be financially worried, what with the present price of sugar. Strange how a cold war with Cuba can make them rich. But I like them. They're progressive. Maybe that's why I like Rhodesia and this company in particular. Those three over there agree that business is for making money and not for inflating egos."

"Are you sure you didn't know they were coming, Guido?"

Here he comes. It's taken him long enough. He looks pale. The drink and the fright I suppose.

"I thought you were pulling my leg."

"I wouldn't do that, Ted."

"I've never seen one that big before."

"Neither had I."

"How the hell did you kill her at night?"

"I shone it up with the lamp. It's illegal but I'm alive and she's not."

Conversations die down. Their attention ripples towards us – even the three people who own all of us in the room except Ted – and the government own him. The gramophone goes on as if nothing has changed.

"They usually spring quicker than a man can fire."

"Not this one. She wasn't quite ready."

"Did the first shot kill her?"

"Yes, but I made sure with the other."

"They have big, horrible claws. I saw a man's leg after it had been ripped by a leopard."

"Do you want to confiscate the gun?"

"No... I came in to get over my fright. I didn't expect to see anything in the truck. I nearly put my face into her claw. You can have the skin. I'll leave your leopard out of my report."

"Thanks. Have another beer?"

"Thanks, I will. I was more frightened seeing it dead than if it had sat up and coughed at me. I often have the fear of being watched at night in the bush. You feel so bloody naked out there in the dark with only him seeing you."

"I've suggested we have a swim afterwards. It's a woman's prerogative to suggest things."

"Yes, that might calm me down. I'd have run but my legs wouldn't let me. What a game warden! You get like this after eleven years. In the middle-time you get complacent but later on you begin to realise how easy it is for him to spring first. Without a gun we humans haven't much strength. Were you frightened, Guido?"

"It's dangerous not to be. Mzenga, give us another round."

The other groups drift back into their own conversations. The heads turn away.

"You don't shoot for the sport?"

"No, not any more. There are few enough natural things left. Meat and protection, that's all. Where there isn't any tsetse they eat cows but here we eat buffalo."

"Have you had enough to drink or can we go and swim?"

"Yes, I'm beginning to have had enough."

"I'll be glad when the rains break. I'll go and change into my two-piece. Come on. Look over there. I can see it better here from the French windows. It's the moon. Why are moons so romantic?"

"Something to do with the spirits. Their needs are drawn out again in the pale fingers of the moon. I was here before any of you came to the sugar estate and remember it well. I first camped over there behind the swimming pool under that mfuti tree. The moon had nothing to reflect on then but the spirits were here."

"You know, Guido, you talk too good English to be an Italian. If there wasn't the accent I wouldn't believe you were foreign."

"Foreign of or to? I'm neither. I'm Rhodesian, African. Out here no one is foreign. People try and make them so but people have always tried to make things different to what they are."

"I'm determined to change for a swim."

"Go on then, we aren't stopping you."

"No... No... I suppose you're not."

. . .

THE ARC LIGHTS shine down from the two msasa trees, from where the branches fork. The light floods the water without piercing it and carves a slice of darkness along the near side.

She has bigger breasts than suggested by her clothes. It is difficult to appreciate the colours of her costume in the violent glare. There is a dark patch at the fork of her thighs that are thick and hard and unlike the slim curves of her legs. We watch each other across the water. Her husband comes out of the changing room. He walks barefoot, wearing black bathing shorts, across the harsh, springy grass that is ant-full in the daytime, into the arc light. Our skins are white, synthetic and colourless. She dives first and I follow. I go down into the smoothness of the water and up again. Surfacing, I swim into the dark slither of night away from the glare and see without being seen.

"It's odd diving into blackness. The water doesn't seem to have any depth."

No one answers him. The three of us watch from the water. The light floods him. My feet move rhythmically as I bend my knees. My head holds almost stationary. I feel her coming closer. She is inside the same area of darkness.

"Sink."

The world holds my movement fixed. My buoyancy falters and water laps over my head. I turn round as I go down and brush my shoulder along her breasts. They feel free from the cloth, pushed away by the soft, warm water. Her hair runs up towards the surface, drawn up by its own trapped air. Her legs float out to me, mine rise and touch and draw them into me and twine – the air presses in my lungs – her legs circle my hips and press me into her – we uncurl and she floats away.

I break surface. Could he see? Now it matters. This is the reality of society, up here. I feel her satisfaction. He still stands, watching the place where we sank into the darkness. I stare away past him at the small, new stars above the club's roof. There is no movement from any of us.

"Aren't you coming in?"

Her voice is suggestive. He dives and water plummets up and down – a black, oily ripple runs over the water and slaps itself around the edge of the pool. I go down into the dark safety. I swim hard and feel the pleasure in pulling back my arms and shoulders against the water. I suppose I should have stayed down by the river.

# 3

"He's drunk and snoring. I gave him a sleeping pill. The doctor prescribed them for me but it doesn't matter. He thought it was an asprin in the dark. Are you surprised to see me?"

"You've only been married three months."

"There's nothing really interesting to do around here except this. I'm bored right through me. I was doing this before I met him in Paris so why should a few words from a magistrate make any difference? I'll still enjoy it with him afterwards. And that's not crude, it's sensible. Life's too short to throw away any chances. We soon become old and unwanted. It'll be the younger people's turn then. Anyway, he let you cite him for your divorce and he wouldn't have done that without any reason."

"You think I should enjoy the joke of giving him back in kind? Jim and I are reasonable friends. The fact he slept with Elio only made me jealous at the time... Strange how you'd never do this in your England but in my Africa it doesn't seem to matter."

"No, I wouldn't have done it so quickly in England but I'd have got to it in the end. It's more exciting here. The first time is always good. I wanted you under the water. Don't feel like that. Jim won't know. If he doesn't know it won't dull his own satisfaction tomorrow, or mine either. I like this sugar estate. I like there being so many men. In London it was all right for the men to be sleeping around. They'd go to a party and pick you up and have you and it was all right when they got home. Why should it be different for us? Well, here I can see that it needn't be different. You men think all of us just want homes, children and security, that the prerogative of wanting 'it' belongs to you. Well, it doesn't. We kid you we don't need it to make you marry us. If we all went around providing it as easily as we all want it there wouldn't be any marriages – no need for them. Most marriages are based on sex and most often men get married because they can't get it regularly. I'm old enough at twenty-seven not to be coy, especially out here in the heat. Otherwise I'm not fit to live with. You'll be doing Jim a favour by calming me down."

"Do you really think like this?"

"I don't know. Maybe I just talk. Maybe when I talk some of what is really inside of me comes out. You have to say something to a man you want and shouldn't have. Can you explain it in words?"

Jim's house is a quarter of a mile away around the other side of the sugar cane outside. There should be a breeze but there isn't. We walk across my lawn. The house will be even hotter inside. The humidity collects and concentrates like a ceiling pressing down. The lacework of the mfuti tree fingers the white fleecy clouds, that don't seem so far above the branches from where I look up at them.

THE SWEET, oily smell of molasses from the cane factory layers the heat and the knowledge of her being here. The drink has something to do with it, me touching her, feeling inside of the silk, three-quarter length wrap. She pushes against me. My hand finds there is nothing on underneath. It's firm and smooth. The curves are pronounced. We move silently into the house. Do I really want her? Talk kills emotion. I shall eventually. I always have done. The silk is easy to push over her shoulders. It clings to her firm, fleshful back as it falls behind.

Our social etiquette forgets and ignores and the needful, basic powers in both of us take what we want and fight to get so as not to be disappointed.

OVER, it has no relevance – will have none until it is needed again – that's in half an hour, maybe less. The first few times are not quickly satisfied. We lie apart from each other on the skins that cover the wooden, block floor in the one big room off the bedrooms. The sweat congeals. She is crucified on the zebra skin, and the dead zebra's fist-ended tail seems to be hers. I know it isn't. Insect sounds impinge on my consciousness and the world of people seeps back into my thoughts. The thoughts are sinful and guiltful but will be overcome when I want her again. A thin, hooded light comes in through the windows in front of me and through the kitchen door, sideways to my left. The furniture and fireplace are indistinct. The kudu fur under me smells of salt and dry skin. I'm glad I can't see anything too clearly. Her head drops over to look at me. My left hand goes out. We join hands.

"It's almost too hot."

"You didn't say that before. I'd like to stand out there naked in the spray."

"You might be cut along with the cane. Have you a hangover?"

"I haven't thought."

"I have and my head's splitting."

"I'll turn on the air conditioning."

"Why don't you have it on all the time?"

"I'm used to the heat. I don't like the change when coming in and out."

"I like Italian men. They're dark."

"It's the sun. Unlike the other Europeans, I spend a lot of time in the bush. I shoot all the meat for the estate and help to keep the elephants and buffalo out of the cane. That's why I've stayed here so long, why I came here in the first place. What I shall do when civilisation finally crushes it into regimented lines, is a problem I refuse to face. My job is incidental – it keeps me here. I have nothing to answer to. Naked on a skin! This is how our ancestors began, the people who copulated down the centuries for you and I. Think of it. If one of them in something B.C. had said 'No, dear, not tonight' or whatever it is they said in those days, we wouldn't have had what we have had tonight. We might even have begun something ourselves."

"No, dear, I'm very careful. I do more than trust the calendar with the pink pills. They certainly are a licence for love. They remove the only obstacle. You don't have the problem of deciding who to make the father when the bulge begins."

"Have you been pregnant?"

"Yes... Twice. Is there a drink in the house? I don't know my way around and I can't see."

"It's safer with the lights out. You are married, you know. What would you like?"

"Gin. A lot of gin and a lot of something. It seems to cure the thirst better than brandy. You'd better put on your trousers. What would we do without fridges?"

"Drink warm bitter lemon."

"Have you the glass firmly?"

"Yes... Thanks. Come down here and sit on the skin and bring me a cigarette. You don't have any regrets?"

"What for?"

"Sleeping with me, Guido. Guido Martelli! I must be able to remember the name in a few years' time. What's the difference between dancing up close and making a complete satisfaction? Especially with the pill. Move over a little. Your shoulders feel nice. Provided it doesn't cause Jim any pain there's no harm. He won't regret anything if he doesn't find out."

"You must make sure he doesn't. The sugar estate is a small place and more than just the animals watch carefully at night. I know at least two women who would wait up to watch us and go home to internal thrills from thinking about it. They're past being wanted by anyone, husbands included. No, I don't regret anything now or before, except I wasn't born out there."

"Where were you born?"

"In Italy."

"Yes, I know, but where in Italy?"

"Why do women always want to know these things? It doesn't matter to you where I was born. The contact between you and me is here and now. I like women who are firm and heavy. I like the thickness of you all over."

"Kiss me then... That's nice. This drink's marvellous. It'll be fun seeing you in the club and knowing what you feel like under the clothes..."

"Who the hell wants to ring the telephone at this time of night? Something must have gone wrong with the plant. They only ring when it's urgent. Often as not I sleep through the telephone. They suspect I disconnect the bell."

"You've forgotten to put on your underpants."

"Hello. This is Martelli. What you want?"

"*Lo umkulu engine.*"

"*Ndinouya.*"

"And the same to you. What was that about."

"You can relax. They expect me to drive myself. The big power house has gone phut. Isn't it nice to have a language that doesn't have a word for an engine?"

"Haven't we time for one more?"

"Sorry, I'm needed. If we get involved we'll forget the time and then they'll come and look for me."

"You'd better put on your underpants."

"You're right. I'd feel uncomfortable without them."

"An Italian would make love."

"Yes, maybe he would. Don't turn on the lights. I'll check for spare lingerie when I get back from the river."

"Do you always take a gun?"

"Always."

"Kiss me."

"I'd like to stay."

# 4

The main chimney juts long and black towards the dome of night up from the depths of the factory. Metal ticking echoes through the endless tin of its inside-lighted shell. Sounds come to me as I pass in the open Land Rover. At the mouth of the factory the floodlit machines sew the sugar-sack tops and others are loaded onto the trucks. The monster coughs out its product there, a continual process day and night, which will go on until the chemical analyst tells us there isn't any more cane to cut with the right percentage of sucrose. The sucrose crystallises and the rest comes out of the factory as dry fibre, which goes back to be burnt in the boilers, or as molasses that is spread on the roads. I don't notice the sweet, sickening smell of the molasses unless I think about it like now. The million-pound factory sits on its hatch of cane. The cane fields go out in all directions, dark and motionless in the night and silent.

This dust road drops straight to the Zambezi. The expanse of water down there suggests a reflection, a mirage, an unreality. The pumping station is in darkness. The standby diesel motors will only have cut in at the factory to keep the crushers and crystallisers operating.

The windscreen, flattened on the bonnet, lets cool air flush over me. I can't hear the factory anymore.

The dark shape of the pumping and power house looms up against the moonless part of the sky and draws the wheels of the Land Rover in. We stop below the concrete walls and the iron stairs that lead up to the first platform. My lights shine at a Land Rover like my own with the name Gokwe Sugar Estate (Pvt.) Ltd. on its door. I turn off the engine and breathe in the full silence of the river for a moment.

"What's the matter, Mnene?"

"I don't know, baas."

He often does but he'll never say, or do anything constructive for that matter, until I tell him and take the responsibility. The dynamos are killers and expensive. I get out, slam the door and stretch my right hand for the iron railing and swing a leg towards the iron rung.

"Do you think it's sabotage?"

"Think it's what?"

"Sabotage."

"Who's that anyway?"

"Jim Marsham, you nit, don't you recognise anything?"

My left foot comes away from the direction of the iron rail and goes back on the sand.

"What are you doing here?"

"In charge of security. The Big Man gave instruction for any breakdowns to be investigated immediately. The shareholders suggested it. Bloody stupid time for things to go wrong when my head's like this. I thought it was Christmas in Gateshead with all those bells ringing in my head, and then I woke a bit further and realised it was the telephone. Aren't you coming up? You took long enough getting here, what kept you?"

"Probably the same bells in my head. You haven't touched anything?"

"My torch doesn't light up much. These dynamos of yours are real big when you get up close to them."

I go up the rungs slowly and get onto the iron gantry that circles the power station. I look out away from the machinery.

"The river looks good. If it wasn't for the hippo, crocs, tigerfish and bilharzia I'd go for a swim afterwards. Swimming in daylight is calculated danger, at night it's suicide. Pity, that. Can I borrow your torch, Mnene? Thanks. Now what have you been doing, you horrible hulks of static modernity? You can go back to the bells at Gateshead, Jim. This wasn't sabotage. Anybody sabotaging up here would have to kill Mnene first and he looks healthy. Have you any idea?"

"No, baas."

"We'll have to strip the control unit in the morning. It's all right, Jim, don't peer. There's nothing wrong with them. I've never heard of three going phut at once. It's in the electric box at control head. How's your hangover?"

"How did you know I had one?"

"Eh... The bells at Gateshead. Well, I'll be getting back. I don't want to fiddle with that until daylight."

"I'll come with you. I'm worried. When the telephone woke me, Stella wasn't in the bed. She's crazy enough to go for a walk at night, but then she doesn't realise she's in Africa. She thinks it's tame here by the river. I wanted to look for her but now we can use the two Land Rovers. You don't mind?"

"I'm sure she'd have gone back if you hadn't woken up."

"Nevertheless, I won't feel any good till I've found her."

"She'll probably be back by now."

"You seem certain. I hope you're right."

"You know what women are. They like to introduce a little drama and self-attention. She probably hoped you'd wake up and find her gone. She wants you to go looking for her. Yes, that's far more likely. She's playing a prank. Does she normally try to pull your leg?"

"No."

"Well, this must be the first."

"Do you mind following in your car? We'll drive to the house first. She may be back. I hope so. Didn't realise I could worry so much about a woman."

He gets into his truck. I follow his path round the gantry and down the iron rungs one after the other and step down onto the ground. How can I stand here so calmly and watch him drive away? It'll be just my luck if he drives round past my house instead of going direct to his own. His headlights will shine straight through the silk and throw her small, round, firm, sex-inviting arse cheeks into relief. Well, if he finds her, she can begin the talking. She came to me. She was better in reality than I'd imagined. I'd have tried to entice her myself eventually. It's the small community, the lack of normal people. Here, feelings become too emphasised. They don't have any perspective to hide among. If he finds her out, and loves her too much, he'll realise his jealousy by physically trying to do me some injury. But even if he does that, the pain will come back to him. Did I feel any of this with Elio? Maybe I did then. It's so irrelevant really. Feelings that have happened are past. Walking and getting into cars like this and gearing like this and moving forward like this bring a reality to conjecture, and make me realise I am alive and here in the Land Rover, and this is all of me here and the emotions outside of me are outside of my control and irrelevant. I accelerate. I enjoy driving at speed over these rough roads. If I knew where the third part of our trio had walked to I would enjoy it more. I did everything before to create the problem and enjoyed it and now I must follow the aftermath.

I slow down to keep behind him as my lights reflect, even at this distance, in the dust his wheels churn up. He goes on and I follow. Should I have any feeling of guilt or fear? Maybe I should. But instead there is excitement. He turns right and goes off direct to his own house.

I bounce the Land Rover along the left fork. The road ahead is dust-free and my lights go on unimpaired. I turn in right and show up the buffalo horns on the side of my house and quickly extinguish the lights. The darkness is friendly. I get out, gently close the door and move quickly across the moonlit lawn. My pupils grow slowly larger. I can see the open door. I walk up the steps of the stoep and look inside.

"That was nice of you to be so quick."

I strain my eyes at the area of voice. Slowly she becomes faintly visible.

"Good God, don't you ever wear any clothes?"

"Not when you're around."

"Sorry. No more. Tonight's finished. Rubbished."

"What's the matter?"

"I met Security Patrol Jim at the powerhouse. He and I are out looking for you right at the moment."

"Lucky you knew where to look."

"Stop giggling. You've got to get out quickly and without even an owl to see you. Vamoose."

"All right, I'm going. Maybe he'll be amorous at the other end."

"Don't you think of anything else?"

"Mostly not. Other things are only incidental to it anyway. How's that for quick dressing? There are advantages in wearing one garment. I'll go out through the kitchen, flit sexily across the road and into the cane and then sneak along in the sugar cane to opposite our house. I'll wait for you to send him off to look in the wrong direction so I can get back into my lawful bed."

"You've done this before?"
"Not exactly. Then it was one unlawful bed for another."
"It's a pity there isn't time."
"Never mind. Life won't end tonight for either of us – or I hope not."

## 5

"Guido, this is Mr. Corbett... And Mr. de Kock. Between the three of us we have a controlling interest in Gokwe Estates (Pvt.) Ltd. Sit down, gentlemen. Is the power operating again?"

"Yes, the modulator burnt out. I replaced it with a new one for twenty-eight pounds."

"It could have been expensive if you hadn't known where to look for the damage."

"I was lucky, Mr. de Kock."

"Your record says you're nearly always lucky."

"Then my luck is very lucky."

The pause continues. His office is heavily furnished and the carpet expensive. Everything in here is opposite to what is outside through the windows. I think the Africa out there ignores all of this, which is sensible.

"You could call it that but this is not the reason why I asked you to meet the shareholders, Guido. Cigarette? You will all have heard that the government is forming a sugar marketing board now that the sale of Rhodesian sugar has reached ten million short tonnes a year. At present we do not have a Commonwealth quota nor one at the United Nations. After Cuba, the UNO quotas were suspended so that when our crop exceeded local demand just afterwards we were able to sell the surplus on a free market. We believe that quotas will come back shortly and then any unconstitutional, governmental act will take us outside the quotas of UNO and the Commonwealth. This, however, is not the end of the road. In the modern world, if a commodity is good and cheap it will sell, it does not need preferences to assist its passage. Not all the sugar-producing countries of the world have international quotas. The Rhodesian Sugar Board is being set up to find a way round the price fixers and to ensure that our political thinking is not coloured by economic consequence. To be successful as an individual or a country it is necessary to be self-sufficient. Other people will only alter their lives to suit you if it suits them as well. The true right of the situation will never influence Western thinking as they only look at the problem within their sphere of interest. They are only interested in a small particle of the problem and yet, unless we think ahead and eliminate their financial power, they can bankrupt us. The rights and wrongs of any internal Rhodesian problem will not even be considered in the ultimate solution that they may force upon us if they have the economical power to do so. World opinion thinks the wind of nationalism is paramount. Modern, civilised, weak mankind must pursue the easy course. But this is digressing. The chairman of the Sugar Board must be able to open the economic doors for our sugar. It is a vital job, which they have asked me to undertake. Mr. Corbett and Mr. de Kock are concerned, as am I, to find a successor for me here as managing director of Gokwe Estates. Without the sugar, I can't sell it. Unless the sugar can be produced cheaply, I can't undersell through the half-open doors.

"Six months ago the growers' association put my name to the government. Since then I have gone to considerable lengths to find my successor for here. It has not been easy. People from outside of Rhodesia are not prepared to take on our problems at the moment. But then I am not sure if I want an outsider. I want an experienced grower and an even better organiser. A man, maybe, who is always lucky. Luck is, of course, the wrong word. Luck can be created by knowledge and meticulous care, by thinking accurately before making a decision. I want a man with great flare for organisation who can maintain an efficient factory and cane production. We have five thousand acres of cane under irrigation, a big area to run smoothly in all its aspects. The other sugar growers are faced with the same management problem, a number of good specialists but no one to coordinate them, so looking at other companies for the man I wanted came to nothing.

"I've had my doubts about your authenticity for a number of years,

Guido. No one has ever known anything about your background. You drifted into the company at its birth and stayed on and even changed your occupation when the previous one became redundant. You must have a strong feeling for the place. You came up to the river to shoot the game in the area, so that the estate could start in a tsetse-free area. When you finished that job you went into the workshop to give a hand, and as we needed someone to keep the elephant and buffalo out of the cane in the dry season we agreed you could stay on in a dual capacity. Then we had difficulty in installing the power house and you just happened to be around to make a layman's suggestion that proved minutely accurate. And then there is your flow of English coupled with the Neapolitan accent. All these things, and many more that I have noticed over the years, don't ring true. They aren't a normal progression in an alternating life. But Africa is a big place and some people come here for reasons they do not discuss. In the early years it was my job to pry into your work and, provided it was good, your personal life was no concern of mine or the company's. Because you didn't have a degree in electrical engineering, or as you said at the time of taking your third job with us, 'just practical knowledge picked up at Kariba', we only pay you half the normal salary for the job. You were happy, so were we and the electrical plant has never functioned better. It was sufficient to see practical results. There was no need to concern myself with your background. But when it comes to top management, we want to know everything. I think my research has provided most of the information. What I learnt and what I know of you, leads me to believe you could do my job if you wished. Just to refresh your memory, Guido, and for the benefit of the others, I'll read a brief history of Mark Harrogate alias Guido Martelli. If you wish to take a swipe at me for prying into your affairs then do so at the end.

"You were born thirty-four years ago in Cambridge, the only son of Gordon Harrogate, the founder-chairman of Harrogate Falls Limited, manufacturers of heavy electrical machinery and components. You went to school at Downside from where you moved to London University. Before going for what proved an honours degree in economics, you did your national service in the army and were commissioned just before your nineteenth birthday. My guess is that between all this your father crammed electrical engineering down your throat. After university you did just one year in your father's factory and then came out to Rhodesia and joined Impresit, the contractors for Kariba, as a gang foreman. I've only approximate dates and movements. I have details of these careers. You must have these yourself."

I suppose it can't have been so difficult for him to find out. My passport gives both names and there's the immigration who gave me a residence permit when I first came to Rhodesia. They knew everything – had it all written down in the appropriate squares. Not that it makes any difference now.

It's quiet in here as the three watch me and wait for an answer. The air conditioning has been turned down too cold. I shiver as I think of it. There must be a clause in the management manual that says all managing directors' offices shall be cold. It makes them more unnatural, medicinal and fitted to their job of efficiency and virile money-making.

"Oh, yes, I had strong reasons. I don't regret ten years of my life, only the previous twenty-four. I wasn't born in Cambridge, though I lived there immediately afterwards. My mother was in Florence when I arrived six weeks before the doctor's calculations. I have dual nationality. After three years at Kariba, speaking little else but Italian and Shona, I found my English contained a lot of the Italian pronunciation and idioms. When I took Rhodesian nationality I also changed my name by deed poll. So to say I am Guido Martelli, born in Italy is perfectly true. I also look dark enough to be Italian, which is a help."

"Does your father know where you are?"

"Oh, yes. He also knows I changed my name. When he learnt I had discarded the 'illustrious' name of Harrogate he refused to have anything to do with me, which was why I did it. Since then he hasn't tried to buy me back to England. Eventually we shall meet as friends instead of employer and employee. I hope so. For me, he had only one fault and that was a need to continually increase his considerable wealth. If he had some purpose for his money I could have understood his reason. But he was only a miser – the modern variety, who builds his wealth in factories and gross sales. There is so much more to what I did that I still don't understand all my motives. I don't understand how my roots of country and heredity could be taken away without any pain and found to flourish immediately in what was then an alien country. Now, I can't even think how it was to be English. I am more physically frightened by what I would have been now as a thirty-four-year-old English executive than anything else. The leopard made me fear last night but not as much as this. The leopard would have created a violent, natural death."

"You left England so as not to be part of your father's business?"

"Yes. I couldn't see any point in a life that took something over that was already made, just to maintain it."

"You would have been very rich."

"This is something I am curious about. What is the desire in people for wanting so much money? The animals, with few exceptions, never kill more than they can eat. If a car is a car, why do people want them so big as to make a bed in? Wealth and happiness are not related. Sufficient food and housing is basic, not wealth. I would have had a very nice life and died at fifty-five of a coronary, frightened to death by the thought of losing some of my fortune. The house would have had numerous bedrooms for strangers to sleep in and the swimming pool would have been larger than anything for fifty miles. I would have had no friends because friendship in business is a sign of weakness, and my wife would have been immaculately groomed and as hard as her nails. I would have spent most of the year running from one closed compartment to another, getting away from the English weather. I would never have been separated from artificiality. I would have trodden on tarmac, ridden in cars, slept on a sprung mattress and breathed exhaust fumes. I don't believe it is possible to be happy in such surroundings. The bush is out there through the window. The bush in England is preserved as a commodity like everything else. But out of that window you'll find the instincts of life that will enable you to be what you are."

"Would running this place be different to running Harrogate Falls Limited?"

"Running the electrical installations is only two jobs back from running the whole of this. Are you offering me a job, Max?"

"Yes. I wouldn't have gone to all this trouble, now would I?"

"You don't expect me to answer just like that?"

"No, I'd think we'd found the wrong man if you did. Worthwhile things must be difficult to get. You'll have to spend some of your time in Salisbury. As managing director you are also in charge of the Salisbury office."

"Naturally."

"You could look at it that way. You'd be living in my house here on the estate."

"I'd prefer to stay in my own. Two bedrooms are still enough for a bachelor."

"It wouldn't look right. The status symbol would not impress the people beneath you."

"Are all people 'beneath' the managing director?"

"On Gokwe Estates, yes."

"I wouldn't want to live in your house. I'd forget who I am."

"I suppose we could make some adjustment, but you'll have to move out of that place you're in now. You're lucky not to have any competitors for the job. Not wanting the symbol of responsibility could change my mind."

"I'll go and do some thinking."

"Let us know tomorrow, Mark."

"Guido. Guido Martelli, born in Italy. Have a look in my passport."

"I already have."

I get up, smile at them and walk to the door, open it clumsily and walk down the corridor to the main entrance. I should have closed their door behind me. The warm air soothes me as I open half of the main doors. I go out and pass their office without looking. They must be hard up for economics degrees to bring mine out of history! I didn't credit Max Rosher with so much of the sleuth. One often likes to think the man above you isn't as bright as he thinks he is. Should I laugh? No... No, it's not humorous. Cry then? The little world of Guido Martelli has gone. The other life has lurched up and looked at him. It still gives me the same surge of sickness when I think of it. This is good. It may mean I was right after all. I tell people and myself that I have no regrets. But this is not true. I want a future like everyone else and though for today and tomorrow meandering around the river is all I want, I know, like the buffalo don't, that there isn't any future. A long, contented summer, ten years long. Even if it remains possible for me to remain in Rhodesia, civilisation will encroach and destroy my peace of mind by the nature of itself. At the moment I can dictate none of my future. I am sucked along by the tide of time and other people.

It's going to rain. The clouds are trying to make themselves bigger than each other. When they get too swollen they burst. It'll cool us all down for a while. That's one thing they can't control for the moment. No, not even that is quite true. In the tobacco areas they fire salt-spray rockets at the clouds to make them rain. Next, they'll make the clouds and push back the sea. Money creates power. Money and power have a purpose. There's purpose in making the clouds rain water. The crops grow. But a larger car is just more difficult to park unless you like speed, and that usually makes you end up bent and tangled in a ditch. I know nothing of the intricacies of running this estate, but I didn't know anything about economics when I went to university. The problem can be understood. The hood of no-knowledge that separates me from the individual facts can be removed with Max's help – clear thought. It's over-humid and hot – will be till it rains. Better to drive down to the river and watch the blobs of rain pockmark the oily face of the river.

I get into the Land Rover. The engine turns with the pressed starter. I wonder if they are standing at the window of his office? I won't give them the pleasure of seeing me turn around. I ease my foot off the clutch and lean into the wheel as the Land Rover moves forward. The T-shaped building, its windows and tin-shod roof recede behind me. The roof tiles broke in transit. The roads were bad then. You expect to see tin in Africa.

The road goes through the housing estate, a spreading, thatch-topped African village that blends with the bush. Between and around everything is the green cane – right out over the sides of the moving bonnet, over the small, foot-high shoots of the new planting and on into the lush, sprayed cane that grows to the foothills of the Zambezi Escarpment. The hills terminate the cane and make a low backdrop for the continual gush-sputterings of the overhead sprayers that flash white water in the quiet distance above the green. I take the quick road. The car and I will go past Jim Marsham's house! My nocturnal habits will have to be curtailed if I accept. Accept! Am I serious to think of it? Flattery has a strong power that makes my stomach flip as I wonder how it would be to have total power over this area of the valley. The world wouldn't be able to encroach without my permission. The whims of my mind would be made into reality. If I could build the financial success of this company, I could extend the power and suck in so much more to maintain it as a reserve against civilisation. I'm thinking too much. The ruts in the road jolt such thoughts out of the top of my head – burp them out.

What timing to catch her picking flowers! Soon the rain will crush their petals. We won't need the sprayers for a couple of days. She did calm my body last night. I am more content with my world today. The disturbance created by frictional life has been sucked out of me. She waves and I wave. We pass each other – one holding flowers and the other a handle of machinery. The dust drifts up to obscure her in my mirror and settles another layer of red on the cane by the side of the track. I accelerate. The dust whirls out faster and higher into the clean, fresh, un-embittered air behind me. Women make a continual problem. This bush, future, Rhodesia, women – problems, all of them. Everything is problems when thought about. Better to bury myself in my two-bedroom house and ignore the outside – run away from the future – or at least stay still in the present.

The rifle, wedged into the pads just this side of the silent windscreen wipers and glass, is smooth to my touch. I take the right fork to the river. My launch is moored by the wooden jetty I built with two of my trackers six years ago. The jetty is rotting now, but can easily be replaced when it falls into the water if I don't happen to be standing on it at the time. The rain shouldn't swamp the boat. If it does, I'll have to swim and hope the crocs are blinded by the rain. If they have any sense they'll go away and come back when the sun shines. Nice to be able to do that in real life. No, not real life – our life – the life of us men and women. I've fished the boat out of the water twice. The first time Kango pulled the plug out while cleaning under the duckboards and after he'd watched the phenomenon of gushing water he couldn't find the hole to bung it up again. The boat gurgled down to the sand, six feet below. The second time a hippo surfaced under us. I'd been surprised for years it hadn't happened but I was even more surprised when it did. The hippo went straight down again without taking the air he'd come up for. The boat sank with him. Kango and I swam for the shore and managed to beat all the crocs to the bank. We had our knives out before the end. I enjoyed it and was laughing when I got out of the water. That was how I lived. There wasn't any thought for a future. I didn't want one really – but then I was younger. We got the launch out by firing the magazine of my rifle into the water and diving for it and fixing a long rope to the stern and pulling gently from the shore with a tractor. The crocs got the message. They look rather wise when you get up close to them.

The trees are just breaking bud before the rains. How do trees produce new growth without any water for eight months? The truck keeps going through the dry bush and the dust behind me keeps lifting and layering itself.

The river looks so inviting, I would like to be placed gently on its smooth, flowing surface and go away with it to eternity, not caring, cushioned by its soft coolness and the quiet of the sun above and hearing the lapping of water as the only sound.

I finally stop the Land Rover above the bank with its armoured nose poised for flight over the river. I get out and the coolness of the water's expanse rushes up to welcome me. It would be nice to stand here and say this will never change. I am a pessimist. The future may never happen.

Death eliminates any future. Without children, who go on into a future for us, there need be no pain or fear for what may happen. No regrets. Regrets for those previous twenty-four years, yes, but not for the last ten. Appreciating that 'now is good' is quite sufficient. Why should I change what I have? Why should I allow flattery to destroy me? To perpetuate? Protection? Security? False hope or sanity? Evolution or destruction? There isn't a correct answer, or at least the correct answer can't be known beforehand – we can only be proved right or wrong afterwards. It isn't possible to stand still, to stop life where it is and expect it to remain the same. Not for us, anyway – the ordinary animals, possibly. Even then I don't know. I can't put my mind of thinking, of appreciating, and understanding sometimes into their minds any more than I can into the future of me. I am frightened to go forward and frightened to stand still. I never schemed for such an offer, never thought of it. We often get given what we don't want. Even what we do want and get, we don't want afterwards. Contradictions! So much comes around and digs me in the back. Here I am now, with thirty-four years gone one way and maybe the same to go the other, and I know nothing. I don't know one little thing about what I want. What I have, I accept and enjoy. Now they've worried me into thinking that even this may be destroyed and that I must decide and do something. I did things when I was younger thinking their achievement would give me what I wanted. I found the doing was exhilarating but the attainment an anti-climax. At twenty-four, I saw where it was leading and I didn't want to go. I remember that first feeling of fear when it came to me. I had been doing all this for 'that' – and I pointed along my father's life and along the lives of most of his friends and saw my ultimate, my goal, my reason for having lived. I can feel it now. How fast I ran and how accurately! Here with nothing is better than there with every comfort. So I tell myself. But my 'educated' mind is trying to disagree with my instincts.

Where is there to go? I sink one haunch, dig at the sand with my fingers and let it run out with the wind. There can't be anything further away from Europe than this bush and river. Here the problem can't overcome me and the solution isn't so important. I'll forget Max Rosher for now and let the spur of the moment give him an answer. Now look at those geese flying out there just above the middle of the river with their necks thrust agonizingly forward and their webbed feet tucked in and just off the water – seven of them in straight flight. For them the white clouds flow upside down on the surface of the river. I stand up, stretch the one leg and walk back to the Land Rover. I lean inside and pull up the rifle from its pads and walk back. I bend for a handful of sand and let it run out in front of me to test the wind's direction and bring up the loaded gun and fire at a clump of debris floating down on the Zambian side. I wait. No splash. I must have hit it. A fishing dugout moves out of the reeds, a little north of the bullet impact. Probably trying to get across to this side. There isn't enough work over there. If he walks on through to South Africa he'll find a better pay packet. I'm wrong – he thinks better and is paddling round towards the 'black' shore. You can't have it all – either pay packets or undisturbed Africa. Civilisation was forced onto us by our circumstances. We couldn't survive, as they will find on the other side of the river, so we went forward – materially, that is. My bullet may starve his stomach but he won't have any education to disturb his mind. Africa was probably right to revolt against civilisation. No, he doesn't care about my gun. He's drifting on downriver. Fishing, that must be it after all. See how often I am wrong about other people!

## 6

The fountains of wisdom spread out from here, from out of the polished, face-reflecting table with its well-carved, bent-up claws at the feet of its legs and the size-shrinking enormity of its length. The alive bodies of five, well-groomed men and me look across its blotting-padded formality, with the sharpened pencils and clean white writing pads at our well-groomed cuffs, into each other's faces. The room is big and *mukwa* panelled and the faces of Gokwe Estate look down on us through her expanding phases to the most recent photograph of the mill. The ceiling is painted in dark crimson.

"Mr. Martelli, will you be kind enough to give the board a brief resume of last year's operations before the balance sheet is discussed."

"Mr. Chairman. Gentlemen. As intimated at our last meeting, the year has been a financial success. We processed just under fifty thousand tonnes of sugar. The average selling price was twenty-nine pounds, eighteen shillings per tonne – we sold as low as twenty-three pounds and as high as forty-five pounds. A static, average level of thirty pounds per tonne seems to have been reached. This is largely due to Mr. Rosher's efforts. We all thank you, Max, not only this board, but the industry as a whole and the country's economy in particular. Our production costs have fallen from eighteen pounds, five shillings a tonne to seventeen pounds, ten shillings despite large increases in wages. A small amount of this was due to a long rainy season which cut our electricity costs. Our field costs have been cut by purchasing a helicopter which has been constantly spraying against cane borer. The number of toppled canes has been negligible and justifies the initial capital cost.

"The number in the labour force is controlled by the cane-cutting operation. When the cane has its correct proportions of sucrose and glucose it must be cut and here, again, the crushing factory has a capacity that must be fed to ensure maximum efficiency. I spent a week at the beginning of this season following the process. The main labour force was right at the beginning in the slashing, Africans chopping at the stalks of cane twice their size – and here I saw a problem. The cane was being cut at various levels, stripped of outside leaf and thrown away from the trash. Either the cane was cut too low and useless wood was passed into the factory, or good cane-juice was being left behind to rot. I also found too many cut lengths of cane that had been accidentally hidden in the trash during cutting. The process was not exact. The waste in lost and badly cut canes was maybe one in a hundred and twenty but these now show up in the balance sheet as a credit of five thousand pounds. This alone was a reasonable reward for one week's work but it wasn't my main reason."

They watch me with money-minded interest. I get out of the plush, fleshy chair and move away from the table and their calculating faces. I look down through the window at the traffic in Jameson Avenue, thirteen storeys below. At these meetings I sometimes walk round them when I talk. My mind works better. The street is wide enough for two sets of oxen to outspan together, without entangling themselves – Cecil Rhodes had practical dreams. The red-flowered hibiscus trees in the park flash brilliantly with the blue sky above and behind them to produce with the white, smooth buildings the regimented cleanliness of civilised order. It is beautiful at first glance – but has no depth of meaning. Now, where was I? Oh yes, Guido, the efficiency expert!

"So you see, gentlemen, a new method of cane cutting was required. This is easily said but I found it very difficult to execute. Here, the matter is clean and full of polished tables and green pads of blotting paper. Out there, way out there, it was full of mud and mosquitoes. The rains had just broken. Slush, trash, and mud. I wallowed in it. I might even say I enjoyed it. For three days I considered how I could reduce the number of cutters but without any result. Then I turned my mind in another direction and considered how I could speed up the cutting. I experimented and found by making them work in pairs I achieved both efficiency and speed. It was necessary to watch individuals carefully, to find two who worked in identical rhythm, and then put them together. One of them cut off the lower trash and severed the cane at the exact level above ground. Apart from letting the weight of his machete fall each side of the cane, he only had one cutting job to think of. As the cane fell, the second cutter caught it and lopped off the top and the surplus trash and threw the clean cane accurately onto a chain stretcher laid out for the pick-up trucks. When the four ends of the parallel chains were brought together, the bundles of cane were symmetrical, easier to handle and took up half the room in the big-sided trailers. The cutters changed over when each position tired. It took three weeks of perseverance to make them work smoothly but when they knew the system, the effect was remarkable. I also saved a tractor driver in eight and a forklift driver in ten. In all, a four per cent reduction in field staff. I gave half of this back by increasing their wages.

"I have been through every process at Gokwe with the same idea. In some I have been successful in making savings, in most I haven't. I am sure that if each of you here had the time to make the same study, you would each in turn think of improvements even after ten people had used their minds to the limit before you. In a business as large as ours, the smallest saving in a major operation can show up as an appreciable amount in the trading and profit and loss accounts. I think this can be said of most complex businesses. There is always room for new thoughts and ideas. This can also be said of life in general but within these walls, you are only interested in money. Outside of them you are interested in how it is spent and that is where we all begin to agree. Yes, a good year, gentlemen. A year in which the ratio of profit to capital invested has been better than ever – the businessman's movement towards perfection. I say 'towards' as he can never reach it – there is no limit to the amount of money that one pound and a few ideas attached to it can make. It is the reason why business is such a successful hobby for the successful – it can always be bettered. Next year we will make more – put that in the minutes, Mr. Secretary, otherwise known as Bob. We must keep our minds fixed on better results. There must be no standing still to savour any success as, while we savour, something will go wrong and we'll start to decay. Balance sheets must show more and more profit each year, otherwise the company is on the road to extinction and the directors are facing the poorhouse. It is all a crusade – a worthwhile need so that society can be improved with its product. The world needs more money to survive. We must think of the whole economy, not only our own selfish interests. This we are doing by increasing the national product. This is what Max has done so much to promote, and so well. We have the chance to make a mark that will be beneficial to many.

"Having said all that, we now come to voting the managing director's bonus. And that's me. Not being a shareholder, it's the only way I get at some of the loot."

"The shareholders discussed this privately, Guido, when I came back from Japan on Thursday. Money is only made by the management and good management is only encouraged by being well paid. We suggest a sum of six thousand pounds in addition to your salary, which next year will be four hundred pounds a month. We are also buying the company a light aircraft which will be at your disposal for personal trips into Salisbury. A second car, garaged in the basement of this building, will be at your disposal together with its chauffeur. A prior telephone call will take him to Mount Hampden airfield in good time for your landing. We want to see more of you in town. If I may be a little personal in the midst of your astonishing first year's success, it would be to say you went back a little too far to nature in your earlier years with the company. We wish you to have the fruits of your work as well as the rewards. There are very few fruits for a civilised man in the Zambezi valley. I believe you once held a pilot's licence?"

"I'm going to laugh, Max. Is there anything you didn't find out about me?"

"No. Now, is the six thousand sufficient?"

"The tax inspector will be pleased."

"I wasn't asking after his pleasure but after yours."

"Yes, Max... Yes, I'm pleased."

"Is there any more business? The agenda claimed the balance sheet was the last point of interest until Guido remembered himself."

"I haven't anything more."

"Good. Is the balance sheet agreed? The auditors have signed. I will add my signature now and ask Guido to do the same. There. We will adjourn. The drinks are behind you as usual, Percy. Please help Mr. de Kock, Guido."

"It will be my pleasure."

"Oh, and Guido, Mr. de Kock is throwing a party tonight. We hope you will come along. You can drive back tomorrow and begin the airstrip."

"Thanks, I'd enjoy a party for a change. I don't know anyone down here. Gokwe can be cut off."

"That's what I thought. You'd better see about lessons to get back your pilot's licence. We want to see you regularly in the capital."

# 7

I get no pleasure out of looking at this. Sitting here without my car lights gives the inside of the company Chevrolet a feeling of security. I can watch what they are doing without them knowing. Stella would like this party. She'd hope to find somebody. Her heart would beat quickly and her feet itch to get out on the gravel and get in there. Later, her efforts would succeed. And I just sit! There's the inevitable floodlit swimming pool and people in brightly coloured, strapless dresses that show their pert knees. The time of the month must be wrong for me. I'm getting old! A few drinks may change me. Why did I say yes last year? It wasn't for this. I think I was frightened. My stomach ached in Max's office as I thought of losing my place in the valley, being torn away from the bush and solitude and peace of mind. I thought I could hold it by taking power. Maybe I can. I must look at this conglomeration of civilisation as the bad side of the coin. The thought of the valley, this effect - has had it for eleven years. All right, I'll get out. It's getting cooler these nights. It won't be so cool in the valley but out of the car and here in the highveld I can feel the winter coming. It belongs to other people as well but when I look up like this at the winter night of dome and star, I think of it as mine.

This will never do. I'm out of the car and staring at the stars. The music from over there is soft and aimed at seduction. I wonder how many of the men will look at the sky tonight instead of down the women's dresses. When I've had a few drinks, I won't think of the stars either. The moon, maybe, but not the stars. Only for the moment am I part of the night sky of comets. If the artificial light came on me now they'd say I was stupid – even embarrassing. Now I'm thinking of them.

The door in front of me across the gravel is open and gaping and valueless in its emptiness. The polished mukwa of the hall throws up the shine of inner lights. I walk towards it and go in. The noise increases as I tread forward to the three wooden steps that lead down to the big lounge that opens out through open, concertina doors onto a veranda that looks drunkenly onto the floodlit pool I could see from the other side. Far beyond is the friendliness of night. The music bumps with the bosoms in the sunken vastness of the polished floor lounge. The drinks are spread out over to my right, on the same level as me, where the diners normally sit as conquerors of the lounge below. The curtains, curled, flood down from the high ceiling though the majesty of their great descent to be dirtied by the polish on the floor. No one notices a thing except themselves and the immediate prospect for their satisfaction. The party is swinging. I go for a drink.

Everything here you can think of and a few you can't. The beers stick their blunt heads out of the ice-filled water in the ice-bath. The labels have floated off stickily and uselessly. I pull out a bottle, pick up the Castle opener by the side of the linen-clothed tin bath and snap under the pressed steel top and lever and feel the suction give. The spent top bounces off the table onto the floor. I kick it underneath and pour the beer slowly into a long lager glass. The froth quivers but holds, and I have what I came for. The band is on the stoep under the big awning that is hiding them from the night. I can see them from here. The lighting is considered just sufficient to see what you've got in drink and women. Ah, the fun is increasing. A young man dives dinner-jacketed into the pool, still clutching his drink glass. He comes up again. Cheers! Bravo my friend. He drinks his chlorine-watered glass as a final salute to sophistication. The others drag him out as the jolly good fellow he is.

Am I being unkind? This beer is full of gas and doesn't go down quickly enough. I am sober. There is little worse than being sober in a room full of drunks.

"Guido! How nice to see you. I'm so glad you could come. You have a drink?"

"Yes, thanks, Max. Looks as though I didn't get here early enough."

"But you'll still be enjoying the party long after they are incapable of doing so. I always find it amusing watching intoxicated people when I'm sober. I learn so much. Drink brings the true person to the surface. I've seen plenty of these parties in my time."

"Looking around, I'd say we must all be a bunch of lechers."

"We probably are. It's the one completely weak spot in every normal man. Come down onto the dance floor. I don't want you to waste any valuable time. There are some exotic creatures here tonight and I've told two of them about you. They wait breathless to meet this man of seclusion! I always add a bit of mystery. It gives them hope of meeting something new. They appear so bored otherwise. I can't stand over-sought women but that's what we have to put up with when they look like that. Quite magnificent isn't she – dressed so openly! Let me introduce you. Henry! Bring Doris over to meet our guest of honour. Doris Whitman, this is Guido Harrogate... I mean Martelli."

"Do you have two names, Mr. Harrogate?"

"No. Only one. Martelli. Guido Martelli. I was born in Italy, the country of sun. So pleased to meet you."

"Isn't he charming, Max?"

"I've heard it said before. Can I leave you together? There are so many people to introduce. Someone always wants to meet someone else. I make a point of remembering and inviting them to the same party. I find it good for business. I'll see you later, Mark."

"Guido, Max. Guido!"

"I'm sorry. Such a silly mistake..."

"Do you dance?"

"Yes, of course. Isn't it funny how men ask if you can dance when they know all along that you can?"

"A little strange, yes. If I translate into Italian I have the actual words for my meaning. What we say is, 'I think you look good enough for bed, do you dance?' You knew what I meant so does it matter what words of English I use? Do you mind, Henry?"

"No... No, you carry on, old boy."

We move away and drift in with the dancing pairs and find ourselves a patch so we can turn and face each other and take hold. She feels sensual as well as looking it.

"That is better, Guido. I like dancing. I like seeing a nice man and then have him put his arms around me like this. You know, Henry does mind me dancing with you. Look at the others. They are dancing so much closer than us. Ah, that is better. In a minute we must get you and me a drink and find a little seclusion. Dancing is nice but even with this amount of light it's so public."

The game of women is exhilarating. However stupid they may be from the outside, the challenge is exciting. The process of seduction is never the same and each move must be made with deliberation and care. There is rarely a second chance in away matches.

"Henry is watching me."

"Oh, I'm sorry. You must go back to your drink with him."

"No. I've decided on you for the moment. I like them to wait."

"And me afterwards?"

"I've never thought of it that way. The waiting person has always been over there somewhere."

"If we go over by the pool, they may throw us in later on. Do you mind getting wet?"

"It's something different to do. I'll have a Cinzano. Isn't it funny looking down on people dancing? The angle doesn't seem right somehow. More than that, please, then you won't have to come back in a hurry. Have a good one yourself. Everyone is much tighter than you are. A few drinks and you won't mind them throwing you into the pool."

"Do you have a job?"

"Yes. It lets me meet people, so I don't mind. I'm a receptionist at one of the tobacco merchants. I think they consider me good for public relations. I get taken out by some of the overseas buyers. I like to see men spend a lot of money on me even though I don't like champagne. One day a rich one will come in who isn't married and who likes me for more than my bust line. Then I may see a little fresh air and less of the half-light of nightclubs. I don't mind it now, but soon I think I'll get bored. I'll find him. You just have to persevere. You don't get anything in this life without aiming for it."

"I'll bring that chair over."

"Don't worry, I'll use the grass. No one will complain at the bits of grass on my dress at this stage of the party. It's nice here isn't it? I like the sound of the water coming out of the dolphin – that and the music. I do like music. That helps me through some of the dull evenings. But you can't tell, you know. The ones who look best are often the worst bores."

"Max said he'd mentioned me to you but I don't think he did."

"No, he didn't. I say, am I making a fool of myself? I took you to be like me, just looking for a chance to make money. It's good to be seen at a place like this on the way up. Are you married?"

"No, but I was. Divorced."

"That happens to most people these days. Are you broke like all the better-lookers?"

"No... No, I wouldn't say that."

"Are you in property?"

"No. I run Gokwe Estates for Max."

"But that place is enormous! You don't look old or hard enough for a job like that."

"Thanks. Maybe I'll soon cultivate the age and hardness. I haven't been trying for long. I'll be glad to get back into the valley tomorrow."

"I get frightened in the bush. You must earn a lot of money."

"Yes, I suppose I do."

"You must pay an awful lot of tax as a bachelor."

"You can look at it that way. But then how much is freedom? Marriage has problems even though it might save some tax."

"Not with that kind of money. You interest me, do you know that?"

"Financially or individually?"

"Both. That's what's so extraordinary."

# 8

"Doris, do you let in anyone with money?"
"Shut up and relax. You men are never thankful. I'm exhausted and so should you be. The amount of energy you put into the last half hour would put most men to sleep for the rest of the night."

"Can't I be curious as I drift off?"

"No. I never mix this with money. Marriage and money is a different story. After you find a lover and live happily ever after."

"This isn't nineteenth-century France."

"No. It's twentieth-century Africa, but where there's a will, Doris can find a way."

"Can I be the lover? I don't like the sound of the husband."

"I worded that badly. With a little more care, I would have got you to propose. A tape recorder could have reminded you the next morning."

"You only met me last night. I might beat you."

"Go to sleep, you're thinking too hard."


IF I MOVE any more silently I'll hurt myself. I woke with the dawn. The morning newspaper is rustling in, pushed under the front door of her flat – a friendly sound. She sleeps well with her mouth shut. One breast is out of the sheets and leans, nipple first, towards me – tempting. There can't be both retreat and satisfaction! Or should I? To nip or not to nip?

The redness juts from a circle of brown that runs into a white smoothness. It is big – and firm. Now, what happened to my pants? Gently lift the blankets and cleverly find the socks – but where are the pants? Ah, what's that? – hers! Trousers over the chair, jacket still in the car if it hasn't been pinched, shirt on, tie in a trouser pocket. I remember – they're down the bed. I'll have to use my shirt tails and leave her the pants as a memento. If she doesn't find them for a couple of days, she'll wonder for weeks who left them. I enjoyed the party after all! There is no doubt that investigating a new woman is one of the better pleasures of life. They do look tempting – the other one is under the sheet but the shape is visible. One fly button missing – I must go in for zips and in the meantime remember to cross my legs when I sit down. I could wake her and propose some mending? No, not a nice way of saying thank you. Bye bye. Oh, she'll be livid when she wakes up in an empty bed. I'm sure she's one of those who like it again in the morning. Come along, Martelli, get out. You'll have yourself talking yourself into permanent trouble. That one pointing at me is very enticing. To the bush!

Now. The door and I have it. Slowly. No noise in the morning silence. The air's cool with the door open and the corridor is smooth with polish. The door closes without any noise. Looked at from up here on the second-floor corridor, the hens don't seem to be properly awake. They sit hunched and expectant, waiting without interest for the new day to get on with itself. The few mealies are growing out of beak-reach. Down the corridor slowly, slowly, as if someone is about to grab me from behind. I have the urge to draw my backside away from the danger. The stairs. Quick – run down the stairs. I run and laughter bubbles up from my stomach without making a sound. I clatter away and out of danger. Into the car. Bang, clunk. Reverse. Wheel round. First gear. Yup, it all smells good, and my jacket hasn't been pinched.

The houses go by. The big trees flanking the road have no movement. It's too early in the morning. Above me, the sky is hazeless and blue, darker down towards the horizon. The air rushes over my head, beaten upwards by the windscreen. The roof is folded in behind the back seat. I do prefer a coupé and especially an Impala Chev – money has its uses. No police at this time of the morning to catch me speeding. Look at that sky – not a blemish. The leaves on the trees are vital from the dew and the red of their flowers are rich and alive. So far, the sun is all good. Left fork at the intersection.

A few more houses. A road sign telling me I'm off to the black North.

That's it. That was Salisbury. Three *dorps* ahead in two hundred miles and then the river. Bushveld. My cruising speed hovers on seventy. I relax.

# 9

As I drop down the escarpment into the valley, the heat pushes into the car and absorbs the sweat from my skin. In a few moments I will grow used to the smell of heat and vegetation and animal.

The road curves and bends and drops and then comes out flat and goes straight into the heat. It doesn't matter about Doris waking up by herself. There can be no claws in my flesh while I remain in this valley. A vast baobab tree tries to burst its girth with age – on my right. Nearer the roadside, I draw towards and flash past a mopane with crackling pods, that has reproduced for thousands of years, bush fires or not. Continually, on either side, gulleys go down into the thornbush. The elephants know that if they stroll across the black, hard road the cars will stop for them like everything else. The elephant has no problems and lives to seventy.

The road continues. A ten-mile road sign flashes past.

The road curves and the car slews with the force which is taking it away from its natural force-line. I take my foot off the accelerator and the power shrinks back into its shell. The brake light goes on behind without me seeing it. The knob on the wheel in front of me flashes in sympathy with the right-hand winker-light. The oil light comes on and goes off again. The car swings heavily across the road and crunches onto the molasses-strewn gravel. This was a good idea of Max's. In business you have to use everything.

The boiler-stack in the centre of the crushing factory points blackly at the blue, cloud-flecked sky above. The distant panorama of green cane swings by slowly. The new cane by the roadside shoots past the car doors. Further and further away the overhead sprays nod the water gently over the vastness and depth of new-green so the water seeps down to the roots underneath. The hills of the escarpment form the limit of my view.

The bottom half of the factory sprawl digs itself out of the cane as I get nearer, faster and faster, and go past it to the river. Glinting in the sun, and way over on my right, the big, single span of the suspension road bridge over the Zambezi grins at the new valley. The road is rutted and wet from a recent spraying... The cane gives way to scrub... The scrub gives way to sand.

I stop the car and get out. The river smells strong and sweet. I walk up and over a sand dune and it's here in front of me, flowing and plopping with fish and grunting with hippo. It hasn't changed. It never has. The water ebbs a few inches up the sand and smooth stones as it flows past me. It flows, yet softly at this time of the year. A mass of movement, spreading and moving together, brushing the islands and banks on both sides, mirroring the cloud-flecks and blueness, grasping its own greatness in its grace of flow, maintaining its mystery and depth and power. I pick up a pebble and throw it out and watch it plop and splash the water.

I turn back and walk up the sand dune. My shoes fill with sand. The car door opens easily. I get in and press the starter and go back powerfully in reverse, turn, and face the car at the sugar cane and sprays. They are cutting cane over to my left.

I didn't take the big house on the hill as the ceilings were too high and the sense of sterility too strong. There was one other house away from the rest that had been used by the managing director in the early days. It has a new tin roof and bush-timber beams. The creepers that tried to crack the glass of its windows are now under control. The original rondavel was built onto three times. The rooms went where the builders went. The lounge level drops down sharply from the rest to follow the kopje. Three steps carved in the rock make a way up from the lounge into the back bedroom where I sleep. At one end of the lounge, by the fireplace, and to the right of the bedroom steps, a hard mount of the original kopje acts as a seat by the fire for the winter nights and log burnings in the grate. The windows are now enlarged. Folding doors give out onto a flagstone veranda that looks down to the oval shape of the new swimming pool. The pool is for exercise. The corners of the veranda are concrete pillars that support my roof garden and the red bougainvillea. I have my breakfast up there in the cool of the first morning and with my beer at night I watch the sun go down behind the silver bridge and get bitten by the mosquitoes.

The back of my house appears more and more as the car climbs and levels out. Creepers cling to the back wall and are growing up the tin pitch of the black roof. The outlines of the roof and creepers are vividly defined by the blueness. The air is alive.

I stop the car and get out. I can just see the bridge through the heat haze. The sun burns at my tan. I lean over the back seat of the car and pull out my swimming trunks, hang them over my shoulder by one finger, squint my eyes to look below the sun and walk around the house and past the corner of the veranda, across the harsh, ant infested kikuyu grass, past the only bed of flowering cactus on my left, over more lawn and tread the hot concrete surround of the pool. I stop, hands on hips, and stare into the coolness of the water.

I slide off my trousers and pants and get into the dark-brown trunks, take off the shirt, kick the clothes away to the lawn and ants, squint out over the sun-scorched valley at the nodding sprays and look down again. I fold into the water. I go down and the coolness embalms me. I come up slowly to break the surface. I just move my feet to keep buoyancy. My right hand is the blade of an oar and turns me to face the house that is darkened by the glare. On the roof garden an angled, multi-coloured sunshade is behind a head and shoulders.

"Is it cool down there?"

The voice is familiar but I can't place it. Ah well, my house is everyone else's. I hope Kango has given him a drink.

"Yes, it is."

I should get out and go down to the office and work. Being away two days lets it build up. There are no Sundays or holidays for the boss. I float out my feet and lie back in the water, my mouth, eyes and nose above the surface at this end and my ten toes sticking up at the other. Maybe I can do the work tomorrow? I wallow over onto my stomach and strike out for the side, touch and turn and swim back. I grab the end with both hands and let my forward movement push me out of the water and twist me round to sit on the concrete, my feet still in the water. I paddle them and kick out trails of water towards the filter plant at the other end, bubbling its cleanliness out of its mermaid's head and flooding it down her tail and into the pool with a smell of chlorine. The sun pulls the drops of water from me. The heat from the concrete comes through my bathing trunks. I pull up my knees and swivel my bare feet onto the grass away from the strip. I put my right hand on a wet patch of concrete and push myself up. Water trickles out of my trunks and looks a little rude if you have that kind of mind. I stretch at the sun, pull back my arms and the flats of my hands squeeze some of the water from my hair. I turn back into the house and walk across the grass, wave at the sun-shadowed figure above me and get my feet on the cool, shadowed flagstone of the step and walk into the depths of its coolness and up the three steps into my bedroom. I take off the wet trunks, dry myself with the hand towel by the basin and get dressed. I feel good now and clean of sweat.

The stoep is cool as I walk out again and over to the iron steps that lead up to the roof garden. I grip the railing and pull myself up. With eight rungs to go, I look over the top. The one has his back to me and the other is a girl of about twenty-two. I don't recognise her. They have a tray of drinks beside them. The ice looks like crystal in its silver bucket, shaded by the awning. Not often do we see women like this in the valley.

"Hello, I see Kango's been looking after you."

"Hello, Mark, I didn't hear you come up the stairs."

"Well, knock me down. What the hell are you doing here?"

"I came to see you. You didn't reply to the letters so this was the only way. This is Gwen, your sister. I don't suppose you remember her. She was ten when you left."

"I find it difficult in normal circumstances to remember faces out of context. Your surroundings as I remember them were not at all like this."

My hand draws a line over everything out there.

"They said you wouldn't be back till tomorrow."

"I always get back as quickly as possible."

"This house is nice. I suppose all the European employees get a place like this. It must compensate a little for living in the sticks. You must all be bored."

"No. I never get bored."

"This house is something, provided it lasts. Gwen's been reading politics and economics at Oxford. She doesn't think you'll be here much longer. It's one of the reasons why we came."

*The Big River* | 49

"Daddy's right, Mark, you haven't any future if you stay."

"They call me Guido."

"I don't think that's important. Look to the north of you and what do you see?"

"Chaos. But why this avalanche of argument so soon?"

"I wasn't considering it from their point of view but from yours. They're all black. Even Kenya. When you were there, Daddy says you wrote to a friend in England suggesting he went out to that part of Africa and in it, despite the rumblings of Mau Mau, you said there would never be an African government."

"I don't recollect any Mau Mau rumblings in this country, but if it starts it won't rumble for long."

"You sound as complacent as the Kenya farmers eleven years ago."

"With one difference, Gwen, we hold the power. In Kenya, it was your government and they were frightened to use it. We've run things around here for forty-one years. The communists have run Russia for only forty-eight."

"And what results from your white domination?"

"Law and order. The right of each individual to progress and live in peace unhindered. The right to maintain an economic stability that at the moment gives every African out there a higher standard of living than any other tribe to the north."

"And with this supremacy you'll produce another South Africa."

"And what is wrong with South Africa?"

"It's a fascist dictatorship."

"To a degree that is true, but then politics must be practical. Theory very rarely works. But for all your country's dislike of South Africa she has prospered where you haven't."

"They exploit Africans."

"And the Africans are paid higher than a Sicilian labourer and their economic prospects are better than anyone's in Africa."

"I don't agree."

"No, and you never will, Gwen."

"But don't you see she's right? It's best to face reality and get out while you can. I'll give you a job. You can name your own salary this time."

"Father, Father, you make the laughter scream up past my tonsils. Do you really want me to give up this for a life like yours? Maybe you couldn't help it but I can. Stay around for a little while. Be my guest. I'll show you my country. I won't try and change your mind. I'll let you change it yourself. Now, excuse me a moment. Kango! No shooting tonight. We have guests! Well, well. Fancy this. One minute you're on your own and the next minute you're surrounded. You know, I've spoilt his day. We've been going out with the guns most evenings for eight years.

"Ah, Kango, you read my thoughts. Put that ice bucket over there and the crushed mint on the floor in the shade of the table. Where did you park your car, Dad?"

"In the garage. Kango helped us. This is a very attractive roof garden. The view is magnificent."

"I redesigned the house myself. Just before, and during the rains, it's too hot. Even a little at this time of the year. I use the roof garden in close cooperation with the swimming pool. Have you a costume, Gwen?"

"Rather. I didn't come to Africa without bringing all that. Dad can borrow one of yours. I could do with a swim right now. Hearing you splash away down there was mouth-watering. Do all the houses have pools?"

"No, only this one and the monstrosity on the hill behind us. There's a larger one at the club for everyone where I socialise. I use this one to keep fit in."

"What's your job on the sugar estate to warrant the pool? Bit of influence with the boss? You always had the knack of getting on with people."

"Yes, you could call it that."

"I could do with a swim. My flesh is flabby after sixty-nine years but if you'll both excuse me, I'll expose it to the sun. You certainly have a tan, Mark."

"The girls at home would fall for that in a big way. You'd have been a real wow at Oxford."

"I get along here."

"But there aren't any women."

"Sometimes, Gwen, I think it is a good thing. For both them and me."

"Doesn't it ever rain in this part of the world?"

"Not for another six months. The air is very dry towards the end, but this is the only discomfort. It's not so bad by the river."

"I'd like to see it."

"I'll take you later on. I'll go down the stairs first and if you fall there'll be me in front of you to cushion the blow. I didn't build this with women in mind. Give me your hand. Now, how's that? Not so bad as it looks. You'll have to do fifty lengths a morning, Dad. All those business lunches have gone to your stomach. So, this is Gwen. I can't say I'd have expected you to look like this. You'll make a sensation at the club. I must keep you away from Jim Marsham."

"Who's he?"

"You'll find out soon enough."

"I'll just go and change."

"Kango, find the baas a costume. You can leave the ice and mint where it is."

"Sure, baas."

"Follow Kango to the bedroom. We only speak English when we have foreigners in the house. We get along better in Shona when we're shooting."

"What do you shoot?"

"Anything. You name anything that's meant to be in Africa and you'll find it out there beyond the sugar cane."

"Does 'anything' come up to the house?"

"If you hear coughing outside your bedroom window, give it the impression you're not there... That didn't take the girl long to change. My, a good figure to go with it as well. Auburn hair and a dark complexion certainly go well with the sun. We have a lot to thank our ancestors for. Oh, and while you're here, you'll have to call me Guido Martelli. No one has heard of Mark Harrogate except Max Rosher – he's the chairman and made it his business to check up on me. So we'll have to come up with a different name for you too."

"I'll race you to the pool."

"Come on in your own time, Dad."

"I think I'll do just that."

She runs ahead of me. Pity they tell me she's a sister. I can recommend her to anyone. Her bottom cheeks move firmly and independently of each other as she runs. The movement stops as she lunges up with one leg bent below the other, hits the water and sprays the stillness with water and sound. She surfaces and slides onto her back, her eyes squinting against the glare of the sun.

"You didn't make a very good race of it."

"I only dive in my shorts when I'm drunk."

"Pretend you're drunk."

So I do. The air inflates my trousers. I swim to the side and shake the water off my face. I get out bedraggled and go around to the filter plant, turn it full on and watch the main spray spurt out of the mermaid and the overflow go shooting down her tail. The sun glints in the flying water. My father dives in. How strange life is. Without him I wouldn't be here. And yet for years I haven't thought of him except as part of some other memory. And yet now here they are, both of them, the two closest relatives I have, unless someone back a while forgot to tell me about children, which is unlikely.

Mother must have been dead for fourteen years – a complete distance that isn't comparable with the present moment and yet without her, too, I would not have lived. All those ancestors too. The chances aren't very encouraging. So there is even more reason when we have life to not let it dribble away. It's too hot in the sun like this for me, let alone for them.

"You mustn't be out in the sun for too long. It doesn't seem to scorch because we're twenty thousand feet above sea level. Sunstroke can make you very sick."

"This is your country, not ours. We'll do as you say."

"You take my word for the weather climate without question, but the political climate provokes a stream of knowledge and certainty! I'll meet you up on the roof garden. The mint should have matured and be ready to meet the gin and soda water. You won't need a towel. By the time you get there you'll be dry."

I walk away. The grass prickles my bare feet and the ants try and crawl up my legs so I walk faster and they don't get a footing – very small feet. Of course, we don't know the political answer but we do know what we don't want and, as we control the army and police, who's to tell us? Economic sanctions haven't worked against South Africa. It'll boom here soon and then all the sharks will come back. I'll have to run up the iron stairs or the soles of my feet will cook. Smells like pork, so they say. The smell of pork is again wafting in the wind of the Congo and the pork is flesh, white flesh under black skin, as there aren't any missionaries anymore, they all got eaten. Everyone in the civilised world knows that Livingstone stopped all that, but when new Africa goes back to old Africa, the spirits of the ancestors are listened to and old, good customs, the ones that made a way of life that worked for them through the dark centuries and led them into little harm, come back again. And what's a little cannibalism after all?

These people in the pool are nothing to do with me now. My roots of life have sunk into a different soil and the taproot is deep.

In the future there will be no need for radicalism as by then the minds will have fused under one sun. This is not wishful thinking. It'll happen as surely as the years go on. No hatred ever stands still. Time crawls over everything.

"You mentioned a mint julep?"

"I was thinking. I hadn't even realised I'd sat down. Dad, pass me the gin bottle and that glass shaker. You're meant to put the whole thing in the icebox, but I just get Kango to plonk the crushed ice and the mint into the shaker. Not too much gin on top of the mint. Two soda waters please. Drink mixing is easy with plenty of helpers. Now, we wait for the temperature to go down. How was the water?"

"Very good. Can't say when I've enjoyed a swim more. Gwen and I only came for a few days, but looking around convinces me I should stay longer. Haven't seen so much sun for years. The works won't founder without me, however much I tell myself it will. Haven't had a holiday for years anyway. Do me good. Is that drink ready, Mark? Here's the top to the shaker but don't shake it, just move it – mustn't bruise the gin. You sure know how to live, son. What car do you drive?"

"If you lean around the end there, you'll see it. We don't want to spoil the juleps by pouring them out too soon."

"They must pay you well. Can you afford a car like that?"

"Yup. I'm afraid I can."

"I run a Jaguar myself. You'll be asking for a big salary from me but never mind. That's a big car. Must eat up the petrol. Stupid, isn't it? On paper you could afford to buy this estate, yet I don't live like this. The black sheep over there doesn't look so black in such surroundings, hey, Gwen?"

"I wouldn't mind living here for three months of the year, if the political situation was stable. I'd miss the theatres and concerts and people for longer periods, but three months would be fine. Isn't that drink ready?"

"Let's try it. The outside seems to be weeping enough. One for Dad... And one for daughter... And one for Guido Martelli."

I hand them round.

"Cheers, son. Nice to see you again."

"I'll be honest, I wouldn't have said the same for you at first sight, but on re-aquaintance I'm beginning to think a family reunion has something. So you came here to convince me I should go back from whence I came. Do you still recommend the transfer?"

"For the sake of the future and any family you may have, yes."

"I'm not married."

"Isn't it time you thought about it?"

"Dad, are all sisters like this? They lecture on politics before going for a swim and tell you to get married afterwards."

"Everyone should get married."

"I know, little sister. I tried it. The experiment was not very successful and lasted exactly five months. Your sister-in-law's name was Elio, just for the record. She came from Madrid and was very hot in bed but not very hot anywhere else. I cited Jim Marsham as correspondent and everything ended amicably. I'm not convinced about marriage any more than I am about leaving Rhodesia. You'll have to think of some better reasons to get me out of here."

"Don't you have any feeling for the country you were born in?"

"Nope."

"I suppose that's clear enough. Are you saving any money?"

"I find it difficult not to. In this job, everything that is expensive is given to me free. I don't own that car. It belongs to Gokwe Estates with the one stipulation that no one else is allowed to drive it but me. This house is theirs under the same scheme. Kango is down on the books as a cane cutter and if you gave him a panga and sent him into the lands he'd hurt himself. I'm supported tax-free even down to my drink bill. What else can I do with my money but leave it in the bank?"

"Who pays for the government, for the roads and police, if you don't levy any taxes?"

"We don't have so many overheads as Britain. You gave nine million pounds to Malawi last month and without any hope of getting a return in the form of trade or anything else material. Just a good neighbourly gift that cost each British wage-earner a pound out of his own pocket. Even more, if you consider the collection costs involved. Gokwe Estates pay taxes and so do I on my actual income. We put up free hospitals and schools for Africans and roads through thousands of miles of bush and still come up with a credit in expenditure and a balance of trade that is 356 million in the black. Too much tax is economically unsound. Provided you can avoid inflation, as we have done in the last five years, the more money that's left to circulate the better. You must encourage people to earn more and work harder. You're being taxed at 19/6d in the pound, Dad, can't be much of an encouragement. No, this is a great country with a lot of sound ideas that we've learnt from your mistakes.

Democracy is weak government and weakness is rotten and goes straight into decay. Why are the Chinese taking the communist lead? Because Russia has achieved stability and weakness is creeping into her policy. Take us. We can't afford to disagree with our government. Difficulties breed effort and it is this that is needed for a country to prosper and prevent the encroachment of decadence.

"There's a little more in the shaker, weaker from the melted ice, but much colder. Now, what has gone wrong at Harrogate Falls Limited so that you can't afford to live as well as me? Aren't your accountants good enough? You want to go and see a tax avoidance expert."

"It's not the money that prevents me living like this. I like living in the country but by living where I like, I see the inside of a train for one sixth of my week. You have so much time to enjoy your money. Business is not, as a matter of fact, as good as it used to or should be. My getting old has something to do with it. I built up the works from the ten thousand my father left me and up till five years ago sales were going up – but not anymore. The government stopping us buying cars on expenses over £2,500 that gave me the opportunity of setting an example of cost-cutting by selling my Bentley and buying the Jaguar. I personally couldn't use any more money but the drop in sales worries me. Harrogate Falls looks big enough now, and would sell for a packet, but I didn't build it up without an intuition, and this has been telling me for months that the slip is growing into a slide. We're not getting into the export markets anymore. German, French and American competition has almost squeezed us from the field and the big and profitable hydroelectric schemes are nearly all in the developing countries such as yours. One of our last big exports was to this very estate."

"I smiled when I saw the name on the dynamos and even more when the engineer tried to install them. You should have sent out an installation expert like the Germans. Luckily the argument was saved by your son being on the spot to give them a hand. I spent a year listening to your theories on power stations for irrigation schemes. It was your pet subject, that and electrics."

"The last time I'd heard of you, you were at Kariba and before that in Kenya. I believe the pumping station and boosters have been a success."

"I looked after them myself for seven years. They've given me headaches. But what about your other products?"

"We never went into home appliances as we should have done and jobbing for factories has never been profitable. We've made parts for everything in our time, big and small, but it's mass production and assembly lines that produce the fifty per cent gross profit. I did get the factory streamlined and economical, but then the unions cut the working week. They've gone off wage increases of late in preference to reducing the time at the workbench. It's difficult to win. Again, the plant's getting out of date. I could spend half a million on new machinery. We make a living, a very good one in fact, but we've been slowly constricting for five years and without new, energetic thought to revolutionise the methods and products, the company will slowly die."

"Is this why you've come all the way to Africa?"

"You got a very good degree at London."

"If I hear that bloody degree mentioned again, I'll scream. Max was so short of talent, he had to dig it out of history last year and now you've exhumed it again. I am not the person who sat those exams. Max's proposition seemed to suit me after I'd thought it out. But I don't run this estate, all of it from the cane to your power station, the sugar laboratory and the crushing factory, with anything but common sense and the knowledge I picked up in seven years by the river. I pick anyone's brains who can help me. My London degree gave me no practical details. It taught me to think, that's all."

"Isn't there anyone here you answer to?"

"No, Dad, there isn't. I'm the *umkulu baas*. The managing director, or whatever you like to call it. All that out there is mine to do with as I will, provided I make more and more money for the shareholders."

"Running Harrogate Falls wouldn't be much bigger than running this?"

"No. Our profit will be close on half a million next year."

"Ours didn't reach that this year."

"But I don't own this place. There's a difference there."

"You can own Harrogate Falls. Yes, it has problems if you want them, that's what I came here to offer you. But I'm glad you've made good on your own."

"I didn't exactly set myself the target. I think I got the job as punishment. I was drifting along very nicely as it was. But one has to grow up. Kango, is there enough lunch for three of us?"

"Yes, baas."

"Give me a shout when it's ready."

"It is ready now, baas. Shall I put beers on the table?"

"Are they very cold?"

"Very solid indeed."

"Let them thaw out a bit."

"They are thawing on the table."

"Thanks... Sorry to shout, Gwen, but that's how we do it here. We've never gone in for discreet little bells and lots of table manners. It may be crude but it saves a lot of time. Shall we go down? The 'chef' says it's ready. I would add that he's better at killing buffalo than cooking it. He stays with me because of the shooting. Cooking isn't a man's job but we men have to get along as best we can."

"There you are, another good reason for getting married."

"I told you, I tried it. Elio couldn't fry an egg, let alone a buffalo steak. I'll go first down the steps. She only had one thing in mind but even that wears thin in the end. We won't eat too much so we can swim afterwards. We eat the big meals when the sun's gone down. My shorts are almost dry. Any moisture gets drawn into the dry air. That's why we let the cane trash lie instead of burning it off. The moisture can't get out so easily. I'll show you round the estate some time if you're interested. But just remember it isn't 'son' showing Dad and sister, but Guido showing around a couple of distant relatives from the European ice cap. It must be cold in England just now?"

"We chose the right time of year to get away."

"You sure did. Now, will Dad sit over there with Gwen on his right? Open the beers, Kango. Even if they have a solid ice centre, the rest will taste all right. Funny this, the family sitting around the same table. Takes me back a few years. I'm glad the reunion is here and not over there. I only left Africa once in ten years and that ended in marrying Elio. Nothing in that holiday was successful. I'm here for good now. The meat looks dark and shrivelled but it is buffalo steak from buffalo shot by Guido. Help yourselves. There isn't any ceremony in this house."

"You'd make a fortune exporting buffalo. This steak is very good for a change. Food can get uninteresting."

"I only eat when I'm hungry, so, whatever it is, I find it interesting. Walking out in the bush at sunrise gets up a good appetite for breakfast. In the hot season I swim at sundown. Why should we export buffalo? It's too good for that. What we have we want to keep, and poison the world instead with a narcotic weed. We don't have to panic ourselves into exports. Our balance of trade must have left Nkrumah and Kenyatta wondering how theirs gets more like yours. Your economists must have an exciting time borrowing money to give most of it away and to keep enough to pay last year's interest. I hear you're giving Zambia twenty million. And I'll tell you something – they won't even thank you for it. They'll grizzle at it not being enough. They'll indignantly explain they have a right to far more as the white man exploited them by building up a mining industry that nets them two hundred million in exports each year! No wonder you can't compete, Dad. No wonder the Germans have you licked with their limited armed forces and no colonies to give away expensively. That interest has to be paid, so the government increases tax and up goes the cost of living, up go your wages and out you go from competing in world markets, Dad. If Britain leaves us alone we'll not only refrain from demanding loans but increase our imports from you by fifty million a year – and that's fifty million you can't afford to lose."

"You make it sound like a maths problem."

"To an extent it is."

"Your steak will get cold."

"Thank you, sister... Why don't you sell Harrogate Falls, Dad?"

So, this is how you look when you've power you're about to lose. His hands shake with the knife and fork. They rattle on the plate. He lifts them and they shake bitterly in the air. I eat at my steak... Put down my cutlery and pour some more beer into his glass.

"I was only joking, Dad."

"Not a very good one."

"Yours must be one of the largest privately owned companies in Britain?"

"It is. I want it to stay like that. It's why I came to plead with you. I want it to stay as it is until I die. What happens then I won't be able to mind about. I've built it. I can't see it crumble away. My brain isn't good like it used to be. I'm making mistakes. I stopped the board agreeing to the manufacture of washing machines five years ago. I'm getting old. Seventy next birthday. I can't take the pace of trains and work anymore. It's why I need you. You have the same blood. With you running the company it'll still be mine. I can't sell it. I would just be an ordinary, rich pensioner. I don't want to go to the theatre six times a week, but I do want to be chairman of Harrogate Falls. It gives me an identity, a purpose. Do you understand what I mean, son?"

"Do I understand you? Yes, some of the way. I understand, too, that I'm glad I came out here. I didn't have ambition or desire for power, so my success here doesn't have the same impediments as yours. I took the power to maintain my security. You want naked power, the power that is tangible to you. I want a say in keeping myself here by the river and in the valley. To an outsider we may have some aims that seem similar, but we know what is inside of us and it's this that's so different. Let the company dwindle. A few million won't make you poor. Get away from it during the winters and live out here. You may even find something to invest in that might tickle your fancy and then you'll be able to build something up again instead of trying to stop a decay. You haven't lost interest in power, but Harrogate Falls no longer sparks your brilliance."

"What would I do with myself here?"

"Relax... And enjoy yourself. You've done enough to look back on. You won't get indigestion eating pleasure. Your kind of power is in money. People lower their pride and bend their knees to money, not the status of management. There are men who'd walk Piccadilly in underpants, and spend a night in jail, for five pounds. The people around you are greedy and give you your sense of power in exchange for money. Have you ever appreciated anything without calculating its price? How would you have considered me if I'd been found in a mud hut by the river? Too many people judge happiness by money. That's why I say come out here and relax. Forget the business world. You can't gain anything more from it."

"It's a habit, a lot of it. I've geared myself to business for so many years that I can't be changed. I can't be made happy by sitting out there by your river or walking around in your bush. I don't know these values. I do know the feeling I get from sitting in a plush leather chair with a clean pad of blotting paper in front of me and time to pit my brains against whoever comes in at my door. I used to enjoy it more but it's age that's depriving me of much and age deprives us of everything in the end. No. I must go back to where I belong. I made it so that I would have to go on living like this many years ago. I'd hoped you'd come back but that can't be helped now. One can only try and change things. So, this is where you've been all these years. You won't have thought of me, but I did of you – a father's privilege. You always retain an interest in something created by yourself. Your mother would be proud of you whether she calculated it in pounds sterling or any other currency of life. You see, Gwen, we must learn to enjoy our stay here, even if it isn't going to turn out as we hoped. Isn't that really what you've been trying to say?"

"Yes... Shall we sit outside? I enjoy my coffee better drinking it on the veranda. It's often fruitless trying to press others into the life we think is best for ourselves. The emotional stress required to make the change is rarely worth the satisfaction of achievement. It's good to look forward with a high degree of expectancy, but it mustn't overrule the present. While we are alive this is how we live. The best must be taken with the worst and enjoyed because this is the only life we can definitely foresee."

Such thoughts are more easily spoken than understood or put into practice. It was easier to live from day to day in the old life by the river but now it has changed.

I drink my coffee and look out at the world I know. It is still and suspended in time. My mind halts its forward movement and registers the immediate. I can't see the sprays. They are underneath the view given to me from the veranda. My mind circles inside itself. It is a soft, self-contained feeling that makes me feel secure and content. A little more persuasion and the heat and food will send me to sleep. But it was better before. I had these moods of solace almost every day. Nowadays my mind is kept too active to let it sleep and rest, to let it uncoil. There are so many pressures on me. Too many problems for me to solve. Like now. How can you tell a man that you think he has wasted his life? You can't. You accept it and accept that his is another life, like so many others, that you wouldn't have liked to live. Anyway, nothing matters now. I am mesmerised by the silence and stillness. No birds, no insects in the midday heat. There is a chink of crockery that adds to my drowsiness – but this is all.

"Are you asleep?"

"Are my eyelids closed?"

"They keep sliding over your eyes to meet each other."

"Help yourself to more coffee. I'm used to being on my own and doing what the fancy takes me. I've no manners. Doesn't matter here. Have some more coffee. Give Dad some too. It's a warm day – the kind that needs to be drowsed through – like the bees, or well-fed lions, or the cattle in the shade of the small trees – they just chew and digest."

# 10

"Stella, you mustn't come when there are guests in the house."

"It's better. He'll never suspect I'm here when you have company."

"He must wake up sometimes."

"We have separate rooms. It has its disadvantages but you can't have it all ways. He probably suspects but so long as he doesn't have proof, we can go on like this forever. I wish you'd let me ask him for a divorce."

"The scandal would lose me my job."

"Yes, that would be silly."

"It's best like this."

"It is nice."

"Yes…"

"I enjoy it as much now as a year ago."

"That's because we never have time for too much."

"The danger adds something to the excitement."

"I keep a revolver clipped under the coffee table in the lounge. They always want to talk first. I can slide it out gently without being noticed. If I'm shot at I want to shoot back, no matter who's in the wrong."

"He's not like that."

"Men become animals when they're jealous, when their pride is bitten into. Even more after living out here."

"He mustn't find out."

"I do like you, see?"

"I MUST GO."

"Is it getting light?"

"No, but the moon has gone. It takes me half an hour to walk back. Lucky I don't have to work in the daytime."

"You're brave to come all this way."

"It's not that. I need it. It's as much for me as for you. I enjoy the walk here but never the one back."

"You must watch out for Africans."

"They never see me. I've grown expert. I know how to move soundlessly at night. Necessity made me stealthy. There isn't any necessity for them to be careful unless they manoeuvre like us. Fun though. I enjoy it. Keeps my vitals electric. Life isn't dull. There is always the last time to savour in secrecy and the next one to tickle my imagination. And that reminds me – I need some more pills. Can you get them in Salisbury next time you go? Send a note round to Angwa – they hold my prescription. It's one of the advantages of being married. They won't give the pills to single girls unless they're irregular. How was the meeting?"

"Fine. Nothing much came up. Max gave a party in the evening but it wasn't a success. I went home early. I don't like civilised crowds drinking cocktails."

"He wants you to get married."

"Who?"

"Max Rosher."

"Maybe... But not to my colleague's wife. Big businessmen are charming so long as you do nothing that loses them money. The scandal of you and me would wreck his staff relationship. Lack of respect for the man above leads to bad work. No, he'd fire me quickly – I wouldn't have any money for you."

"Haven't you saved any?"

"Yes, but we couldn't live for long at the right standard on six thousand pounds."

"You could get another well-paid job."

"I wouldn't want one if it was outside of this valley."

"You make things difficult."

"I'll get the pills for you. An enlarging stomach won't help our cause."

"I'll go now. Kiss me.
"Umm..."
"And again."
"I agree – it's good."
"Cross fingers for me."
"What for?"
"In case I meet him when I get back to the house."
"You'll have to lie where you've been."
"And keep away from the lights so he can't see the smirk on my face."
"Something like that... Good night."

"Jim, Stella, I want you to meet some distant relatives of mine. This is Gwen Harrogate and her father, Percy Harrogate."

"I heard you had friends at the house. Didn't know you had any English relatives. Did you, Stella?"

"No... No, I didn't."

"Glad to meet you both. I've known Guido for a long time. We'd be pretty intimate friends you'd say. He cited me for his divorce – it was the only way he could get one quickly. I didn't even know Elio outside of a drink like this, but you have to help out your friends."

"You were more than obliging, Jim. Very helpful in fact, but it's not the kind of thing one mentions to people direct from England. They don't like to accept the vulgar undertones of life."

Both father and sister look uncomfortable as we sit back into our chairs. I should have ignored his remark instead of making it worse but that's how I'm made. I don't look at Stella. We have accustomed ourselves not to exchange any emotion in public. Any strong communication, however short or flashed, can be intercepted and understood by others. At some future date minds will exchange thought without any conversation.

The club is quiet. The sun begins to go down behind us. The changing colours are mirrored in the swimming pool, and bleach the complexions to thin-skinned, evening facings. We sit on plastic slatted chairs. The voices fall as the day goes down. Mosquitoes feed on the blood of humans that haven't grown used to the needle-bites. So much is in the evening – a whole sadness of life going down. The morning will bring new hope but this going day will have gone forever. Our earth is almost ready to show us its one side of darkness. The clandestine, the unseen, will come out into the colourless night with shadows and human sightlessness. This is how we live.

The cicadas zing individually… More of them join to be lost in the greater Africa. The sky colours. The shuttering lightlessness comes down in the east. The rim of the sun begins its slide away into violent redness and leaves the fading light to be chewed up by the eastern night of vermillion and dark pilot-black-blue. The dusk hangs. The in-between it is now, neither one thing nor the other. The colours change again as the sun concentrates its last resort of violent, molten yellow that shrinks to its orange core. The greater universe, like the screen of heaven, stares down at us. What does it know about us? It is friendly to me, yet awful, beyond my comprehension as to its depth and hidden meaning. In front, the stark trees stand like soldiers on the crown of the escarpment and march both ways from the sunken sun into the night, all blue and mauve and darkness under the stars. The pastel colours subside to go down to join the sun. The moon picks up brightness, and the noise of the cicadas. Bullfrogs croak loudly from the swimming pool and others plop onto the hard water. It will take a while for the embers to die down behind the escarpment.

Now is the time for fear. I grow alert so as to be able to combat the devil.

"Beautiful, isn't it, Gwen?" So strange to have a sister after all.

"Were you watching as well?"

"I always do when I have the chance."

"Be careful, my dear, or he'll be telling you all about the moon. He may be the boss but he won't have changed inside of him. He was and is a ladies' man."

"I can handle him, Jim."

I look from her and then back to Jim. I turn to Stella who wants to speak.

"Why do you always bring this up? I'm sick of it. You used to be what you call a 'ladies' man' before you married me."

"I haven't changed – don't accuse me of that – and, anyway, you are the one who should know."

"I suppose you're jealous of Guido for being free to do what he likes."

"I do as I like."

"You must be better at secrecy than lying."

"Take no notice, Gwen, we often talk like this at the club. It doesn't mean a thing. Guido will tell you."

Now does he know or doesn't he? I am looking for danger. It could be my imagination.

My father sits back from us and listens to the surface of our conversation. Does he regret his youth? Does this fear of age remain so dominant when one has it... or does the reality make it acceptable? How old he looks after these ten years. I have noticed little change in the mirror. People say I look thirty-five – ten years older. These affairs ration my virility and bachelorhood. A thirty-five-year-old man with a child of twelve is a whole generation older than me. I retain the old hobbies and forget to recognise the new face that has grown onto the one I brought with me to Africa. I don't have to worry about marriage now because she is married already. One danger counters another! I don't regret having my own company for most of the day but not the night. It is this need that makes many a home. It certainly makes Jim's. How will he react when he finds out? I have never seen the depths of his pride. Maybe I will. I don't have this need to express myself in children. I don't want a stable life or one etched with the cement of security. I enjoy danger. I look forward to fighting for a living. I hope the eventuality will force itself upon me again. To remain static is to decay. A decayed mind is more useless to oneself than the people who have to listen to it. To plan ahead for more than three months is tantamount to killing my excitement in living. I like to explore life. Landscape gardening it into regimented rows is a disaster of permanent monotony.

I sit here a little straighter than I used to twelve months ago. It is part of my new, outward approach that goes with the job. People don't work properly for a man they talk to comfortably. I don't have to maintain the façade in the bush or at night with Stella. She knows too much of how I really am but this is the price of pleasure. It would have been better to remain as I was in the old job but it is rarely possible to stay still in any life. I live where I want even if the subconscious minds of the people I work with fear me for my power over their future. Most of them need a future – it is important to them. I do the new job as well as I can, as it gives my mind something to immerse itself into and something to sharpen its ability on. When I have solved most of the problems I shall grow bored and this has always been the case for me. For now I sit and listen and drink while the mosquitoes buzz for the softer, English flesh beside me. It isn't early enough for bed but after last night I could do with some sleep. Normally I nap at lunchtime but guests that have been asleep all night prevent such things.

The bartender moves into my line of vision. He looks at me expectantly with the arc lights catching in the whites of his eyes. His black skin shines.

"Bring us another round."

Why should I disappoint him? He thinks it will help his career if he serves me. Maybe it will. Who knows? Who knows how I will be in five years' time. The job may change me instead of me changing it. I may become a normal boss and favour the people who inflate my ego. What a repulsive thought. I shall be forty then. More than halfway gone. And then what?

There are four people here – a husband of a mistress, a mistress, a father and a sister and each of us are more important to ourselves than to the others. Other people, countries, universes only have relevance through the way they affect us. They don't exist for me unless seen through my eyes and if not seen, they don't exist at all. So the daily cycle continues its revolutions and goes out from me and grows weaker with the distance. I do feel a vital existence when I go into the bush alone. I look into myself and see the world of existence in me. I want life then and take it, without any hankering for another set of circumstances. It is a pure existence without any sediment of society to billow up and shroud the issue of life. In the bush I am balanced on my own emotions, reliant on nothing but my own life.

This, now, is wrong. I have no feeling for her. I can hear the ridicule shouting out of myself. She isn't what I want, yet I want women. But there isn't anyone in my life now or before who can give it to me. And solitude is not enough. I want this 'more', this completion. Drink kills it for a while and the next day finds the searching hitting out at my body the harder for having been pushed aside and aggravated by the alcohol. Where do I hurl myself to find what I need?

There needs to be emotion in sex or otherwise the satisfaction is brittle and baseless, and the building process of tension rises like sap in me and cries to get out, fights and fights me for an exit and ends up lodged in my stomach as hard and violent as death itself. The bush calms me down, but will it always? Is it enough for me now, here, in this moonless anonymity, clutched around by the night and other people's conversation? Will the need crash out and send the balance of my mind away from the infinity I look to for completion? I have all the materialism but without understanding, and the satisfying of my own self, it is nothing. No job, no peace, no rest. She must 'be'. No wishful thinking.

Reality. It is this I see. There is no means of looking, either. I must wait – like now – sit here and hold myself in – tighten all my bones and skin to stop the danger going out of me uncontrolled.

It's this new life – the drink and smoke and false people falsifying to comply – the restriction of my liberty – the curtailment of my emotion so it is contracted and contrived, pushed and scuttled into a form that makes me like this. I'm violent. The sun's gone and the night's here and this is how I am. I don't have to hide, only to pay for the drinks. They can't see me. Ha ha. There is it. The rub. Not seen, not cared for, not caught, not guilty. Guilty of what? What have I done wrong? Nothing... Nothing... But I must hide it. I am not allowed to understand and to live by this understanding. I have been made to want like all others. I have joined the sick array of humanity and become like them, no longer like the bush, no longer as I was meant to be, as I was, could have stayed as but didn't.

"Excuse me for a moment. I don't feel well."

"Can I get you something?"

"No thanks, Stella. Look after my friends, Jim."

I go away from them – quicken my pace – go behind the club and out of the forced light and into my car. I drive away, quietly but certain of my intent. I turn off to the river and follow the track, blazed and splashed by my lights. I look in the glove compartment. It is there – cold and steel. The moon is thin and pales the light now, pales it without contrast. I go too fast but it doesn't matter. The river comes out of the night to me. I brake and slew round to a stop on the bank above the gliding, moon-paled water that only has a surface. The engine and lights cut out. I open the door and get away from the machinery. I throw off my shirt, shoes and socks, and go on down to the water in shorts and pants. Me, this, the knife and water. The moon maybe too, but mainly the river and I. The sand in my toes. Harsh rocks hidden that tear at my soles. The knife pointing from my right hand and the river coming closer. I refuse my ears the right to listen to anything but the emotions that must be crushed. I go in, and in and in. The water comes over my body. The crocs are here. The garfish too with inch-long teeth. I dive in and go under the black surface to blackness. The water explodes in my ears, presses, hurts and the water crushes all of me. I surface and gasp for air as I am lugged away down the stream – debris like the weeds and flotsam, part of the tide. I strike hard for the shore. The flat knife thrust into the water jerks it from my hand. I flounder for the shore. Something brushes my body but I hurl myself on against the tide and river. I want to live. The shore creeps in. Too slowly. I fight even harder and crash my hands onto a rock, grip it, clutch it, and drag myself away from the tide and into the shallow water. Sand. New energy, new power. I emerge from the water and crawl away from immediate danger. The crocs slink far away. I sink, exhausted, free of any emotion but tiredness.

The night remains static. Air heaves into my lungs. The dry sand clings to my wet skin. The river will be flowing just the same. I turn onto my back. My eyes focus and the mopane branches extract themselves from the whole night and stand out alone between me and the moon. The moon is between me and something greater, and further still is infinity. Look how far I am from this, how little I comprehend with so little here and so much space out there – all the distance between me and the infinity which could be understanding. Maybe my instinct understands the reason for life but instinct is like so many of the other parts of me that I have no control over.

Reality returns but without any pain this time. I want to walk and walk and go further with myself into the hard, dry sticks and trees and long grass. I don't want their life. I want to live and not be lived. I can go. Now if I want to. But with this problem of women. I will go back. They don't see me. No one does. My shell has been camouflaged for twenty-five years, through all the time of my conformity. Eventually I will die but for now I must live. Women. I listen to its need – not with excitement but fear. Before, I could track the buffalo and kill him and come back tired, but satisfied. I slept after all those hunts without images damaging the balance of brain tissues and preparing the ultimate chasm of nervous disorder for me to fall into. For a year, now, my brain has been crowded by needs and frustrations that have led me here. There was more to this rush into the river than I am able to understand. I have so many things and yet I have grown unstable inside of myself and crave another person to complete the roundness of my personality and make it whole. It is the one important step forward in my life that I have not yet taken.

I can remember camping here with Kango and wanting nothing but the feel of my gun lying beside me and the moving shadows caused by a good fire, a full stomach and the chorus of night Africa around me.

I must get up and walk along the river to my car. The river took me down a long way. I feel more naked than my lack of shirt and shoes suggest. My ears strain into the bush, away from the river. I get up and begin the walk upstream. My nostrils analyse the scents of night, prying the dangerous from the gentle. My eyes grasp movement. The hippos are grazing along the Zambian shore. Hear them! They move heavily. They can run as fast as me, their short, trunk legs moving like a horse's, their ugly heads bent on protection of the small dog-sized hippo that are their children. The light from the moon and stars is stronger. There is a galaxy to my right, above me and the trees, that is lace. The air is cool and fresh from touching the river. It goes into my lungs and eliminates the swim and the lost knife sinking further and further from my grasp.

I walk and the night goes with me, restoring my sanity. Even without a gun I can be master here. My instinct can match theirs. I don't relax my surveillance but enjoy it instead, enjoying straining myself to remain alive and breathe the river-fresh air. It is here I feel like a king, not on the estate or in the boardroom. Here, I am the prince of myself. Each sound is familiar. The insect noises come to me separate from the night birds. The animal noises I hear from individuals. Croaking frogs are loud in the river. The night goes on and the river flows. An owl crashes away to my left and the bush squawks at its errant manners. I smile and put back my heart in its place. My body walks on, with the big, ungainly bird moving away in the air without a sound or hoot. I walk up into the trees and follow the game track.

Time and distance dissolve into the rhythmic movement of my feet.

Subconsciously I size each tree as I come to it and gauge the quickest way up its trunk.

THE CAR IS AHEAD through the motionless outline of grass and trees. There is no colour, only black and white. I walk to it and grip the metal door, push down, open and get in.

## 11

"Hello. The club? This is Martelli. Give Mr. Marsham a message. Ask him to bring my guests to my house when they are ready for dinner. I've been detained waiting for a telephone call. Thank you."

If I'd asked that eighteen months ago there would have been an argument. Max's fixed-time call from Geneva is opportune. I refuse to let my mind look any further into my future. I don't like what I see so I won't look again until my emotions drag me down to where I have just been. The car and this house, the necessity of picking up the telephone and accepting the fixed-time call, have again replaced my props of society and brought me back to familiar objects and habits. Familiarity breeds a false security.

"I'm sorry I left you both at the club. Thanks for bringing them back, Jim. Max is coming through from Geneva on the telephone at seven fifteen but the exchange keep you hanging around in case they have difficulty getting through."

"How do you feel?"

"Much better now. We'll eat when the call's come through."

"How did your hair get wet?"

"Eh... Women notice everything. I had a swim in the pool. We may come down to the club later, Jim. We'll see you then. Give my regards to Stella."

"See you later."

"Yes, that's the idea. And thank you again… Now, what are you two going to drink? Anything you want is either in the cocktail cabinet or Kango will bring it. I hope the mosquitoes weren't too bad. They've been persistent this year."

"Why didn't you ask him in for a drink?"

"Ask your father. Here, the boss is 'boss' all the time. Jim may be a friend but every now and again it's necessary to remind him of his employee status. It's one of the rules of management. I don't like it but it is there and has to be done to remain at the top of an organisation as large as this. They don't expect me to get familiar with anyone who is not on the board. I can get drunk in Rome and lech there with as many women as I like, as this is what they expect me to spend my money on. But do the same thing right here and they'll laugh at you and then the fall is faster than the decline."

"Who is Max?"

"A very rich man. He owns thirty-four per cent of the company. He probably wants me to hurry through an order for him on one of his new clients. He prefers me to chase the Sugar Board as he thinks I have more to lose if something goes wrong and he's inconvenienced."

"Is he married?"

"Twice, I think."

"All the men are married here. I think Jim is just marvellous to look at. I don't like his wife."

"People often marry their opposites. I think Jim liked the look of you and his wife didn't. You can't be friends with everyone."

"Did he really seduce your wife?"

"I don't think she needed much seducing. She came easily to me. I was young then. I'd been in the bush too long. I didn't have the required confidence till afterwards, so I married her and found her as easy with others, and that anyway she wasn't as satisfying as I'd led myself to believe. If Jim didn't seduce her he missed a very good opportunity."

"Have you tried to pay him back in kind?"

"What do you mean?"

"By having an affair with his wife."

"Father, help me out of this! Where do these modern young girls manage to find so many dirty ideas?"

"That's how they are these days. I've given up trying to influence her."

"Stella likes you, you know."

"So do you, I hope, but it doesn't mean we're having an affair even though they don't know you're my sister."

"No, there's something else between you and Stella. You look too smug sitting next to each other."

"You must have a good imagination."

"I wouldn't mind imagining him without a wife. Maybe we should get together on this one."

"Pretty girls always want what they can't have, or at least can have but shouldn't. Married men have this attraction for them. It seems to stimulate their masochistic tendencies and drops them deeply into a trough of self-pity at having found that what they want, they can't have. The emotions flood out in tears and gratitude for so much self-sorrow. Some men have the same problems."

"You're looking at life with a strange slant. It's too much Africa that has done it – you don't belong here so it makes you peculiar for forcing yourself into its company."

"You're wrong. Africa welcomes new people. She's been doing this all her life and she particularly took a liking to me. My slant has become different, yes, and not only because I'm eleven years older. I have drawn my companionship from the bush and subconsciously the African people. Their lives and accents have grown into my life and changed me. At the time, I was not conscious of the change or the fact that when I became lonely or disappointed with life I ran out with a gun into the bush to be reassured and made whole again. These things are part of me now, me the different person. The bush enabled me to extract myself from the emotions of other people so I could see myself related to myself. The image I saw was clear, if nothing else. Having been able to isolate the problem of myself I could look at it and decide what to do. I could see what I really needed to give me happiness. And, though I can't yet control them, I can see the situations and contexts which can overpower me. I can see in my life what I want and what I don't.

"Instinct is not impulsive. It is the motive force of our existences and like any other motive force it can be comprehended so that we know beforehand how we will react to our lives. There are exceptions to any rule because the rules are never understood completely. They taught you philosophy at Oxford by making you read and analyse the lives of other people and their understanding of life. This may end by producing for you a large knowledge of the generalities of other people and the generalities of one's own life. But what are we really trying to understand? It's nice to understand something of other people but isn't this incidental? Self is the important unknown and self can only be understood by looking into one's own mind. This I have been able to do in Africa and because of this I have found many hours of complete happiness. I can look back on the last eleven years and say that I have been in a state of happiness half the time. If you became able to go back, both of you, over the same period to tick off each hour of woken happiness not stimulated by artificial entertainment, you'd find it hard to find five and a half years of time. Some people look back on their lives and count the peace in weeks not years. So, here is Africa. All of it out there, most of it unspoilt and therefore real.

"Take some of that mosquito ointment, rub it on the exposed parts of yourselves and we'll go up on the roof. I'll hear the telephone from there. Kango! Bring some ice and the drinks tray up top. Bring my gun as well.

"Sometimes I see elephant in the cane and like to have something close at hand to frighten them off with. Here there is always the possibility of some excitement just around the corner."

She smears the ointment over her white arms and neck. My father is more surreptitious but just as thorough. I only use the ointment down by the river just before the rains when the mosquitoes blacken the arms and face. To me, the noise is more irritating than the bites. There is a breeze out here. Any movement of air in the valley is felt on this hill. Is it really the same night that took me into the river? Nothing has changed out there. The night, if anything, is even more clear and brilliant. Kango comes up the stairs behind us with the drinks and the gun. The shaker is a quarter full of fresh lime juice. I add two tots of gin and a splash of Cointreau, top it up from the soda siphon and plop in eight chunks of ice. Kango knows the kind of drinks I like when I go up on the roof. A long, lime drink goes well with the night and the surprise freshness up here. I let the ice seep coolness into the lime and gin.

They are both silenced by the aura of the great expanse which is right around us. There is nothing hidden. No clouds. The sky goes on forever. The world can be seen to the limit of the valley, shaped by darkness and backed by the clarity of the endless heavens. The silhouetted barrel of my gun juts violently at the night, where it leans against the roof railing. The small yellow light by the table doesn't penetrate further than the cooling drink and waiting, cut crystal glasses.

The night is stronger than anything else. I scan out over the sugar cane for any large, dark mass that moves. Normal, night noises come up to me. I get up from the wrought iron chair and go over to the drinks. Over this side I can see the factory with its phallic chimney jutting from the pinpoints of lights. The hum of machinery comes to me when I think about it. The noise is constant all the year and so unnoticeable. This is our world and we understand it as the serfs understood their groups of hovels, their villages, their homes, the area of land that was theirs. We know what is here and where we can walk with safety and we know that the river is dangerous at night.

They talk among themselves and I listen without hearing anything. Their conversation of 'home' is as foreign to me as the elephant gun over there is to them. My mind fugs in the warmth and pleasure of standing here with one foot on the rail. The river has again made me aware of what I have. Yes, I'd like to be out of this job but if I remain free of contamination I can come back to feeling like this. The drinks will be cold enough by now. I smile encouragement at their conversation only to realise it is too dark for them to see. The creases in my face go back to normal. I stir the liquid in the shaker, press on its silver top and pour into the first glass, cut back and move to the second. The telephone rings sharply from downstairs. I fill the second glass quickly. The party line rings again for me, three shorts for the boss.

"Here's yours, Gwen. How's that for you, Dad? Excuse me. That's my call. I'll be back in a moment."

I move quickly across the roof to the iron stairs. Awkwardly, I go down them three at a time and hit my elbow before leaping the last six steps. Three short rings again. Into the house from the veranda and on into the hall, flicking on the light as I pass the switch. I pick up the telephone.

"Martelli."

"Long distance call, sir, for Mr. Guido Martelli."

"That's me."

"The line isn't good. You'll have to speak up."

"Hello. Hello."

"Max here, can you hear me?"

"Just. It's a long way to Geneva from Gokwe Estates."

"Everything all right at your end?"

"Yes, thanks. The borer have got into one land but we haven't lost all that much cane. Can you hear me?"

"Not so well... borer... expect them any time."

"I can't hear."

"My... is bringing... I want you to meet them at... airport."

"Your who is where?"

"My daughter. She's going back on holiday, it's her nineteenth birthday soon. Can you hear?"

"I can now. It's cleared."

"She's bringing back a girlfriend with her who's never been to Africa before. I'm not coming back for two weeks myself and this is the only plane I can get them on. Everyone suddenly is going to Africa. I wouldn't trust the two girls in Salisbury alone. They're too young with too many ideas of their own. Put them up on the estate with Jim Marsham and his wife. They can't get into any harm there by themselves in the bush. I'll come up and relieve you of them when I get back."

"When and where do I meet them?"

"Salisbury Airport, tomorrow. Scheduled ten-thirty on flight G5 via Jo'burg from Geneva. They've left already."

"How's the price of sugar over there?"

"Bloody horrible but we'll still make a profit. We can grow it at home cheap enough so I'm underselling all the other bastards even if there is a surplus on the market. You keep growing it and Max'll find someone to sell it to. Now, you got what I want. These calls cost money. I don't want either of them to get into trouble, see. I hold you responsible. See you, Guido."

"Okay, Max, see you."

So, I'm now a kindergarten for teenagers!

I slap the phone down on its hook and walk back, flicking off the light as I pass along the corridor, into the lounge and out through the veranda into the night air, walk round and grip the iron rail and go up smooth three at a time.

"Has the market crashed, son?"

"If it did, that man would pick up all the pieces and put them together again even more to his liking! We're selling cheap but still selling, which is more than most of the producers can afford to do at these prices. No, his teenage daughter is flying in tomorrow and I'm to act as chaperone."

"It should amuse Jim, the idea of you being a chaperone."

"His morals are no better. Max gives me these jobs thinking I won't put a foot wrong as he controls my job. He thinks money is God and judges everyone else by his own standards."

"I never got that bad. In fact, it wasn't money I was after if I think back, but power. I just wanted to control something as big as Harrogate Falls. It's a great satisfaction achieving the ambition of one's life. That's why I want to hold on. But life often won't give us the last bit. If I die, sell the company, Gwen. It'll be yours for all intents and purposes as I don't think this bush-rotten son of mine will want it even for the cash he can sell it for."

"I'll have to leave as the sun rises tomorrow. The plane gets in at ten-thirty. Can you look after yourselves? I'll organise a driver and a Land Rover for you. Kango can go too and show you some of the valley. He knows it as well as me. He's very accurate with a rifle but leaves the pistol shooting to me. You have to squeeze when the gun's still in the holster and pointing at your toe so by the time the gun gets out and is levelled, the hammer has gone back and come down on the cap to send off the bullet. He thinks I'm going to shoot off my foot someday. Maybe I will. There's enough here for three more drinks. How are your glasses?"

"Empty."

"That's it. You're getting into the ways we lead out here."

## 12

*I* am completely awake. Thought jerks me fully to reality and my faculties are as good as new. The night is thinning out. I can just see the windowsill. I throw off the one sheet and walk naked to the window. Lean into the clear dawn. Over to my left the beginning of light is picking out the sky behind the escarpment. I watch and wait. I have this much time. The coolness after the sheet covering invigorates and makes me feel even better. I'm not thirty-five. This isn't possible. Like a small boy up for a dawn shoot with his father! This is more like it. Hold the world! The beam of scarlet slips up over the mountains. The sun is born. My little-boy's excitement wells up in me and my satisfaction at being alive is overpowering. I want to get out of this window and into the morning. It's an emotion society dictates a grown man shouldn't talk about so I enjoy it even more for having it to myself. Who cares what the world thinks? It's what I think and for me that's important. The new, blood-red glow seeps higher and wider above the hills that are growing depth within themselves. Jagged projections come out of the night again, the red and yellow, paling and paling out further to blackness. I turn back and walk into the bathroom and straight on into the shower to pull the lever marked 'cold'. A pause and water gushes away the last of my close-contaminated sleep. The freshness gets me out and I rub myself dry with a coarse towel. Next are my teeth – I scrub them with soap, a legacy from my first days in the bush when toothpaste was only to be had at the end of a three-day journey – slick on a dash of water to my hair – a quick flash with a long comb and here we are, naked but ready for anything.

The dawn light has found such things as my slippers on the bedroom floor and the black monkey-rug. I open the big built-in cupboard and get out a polo shirt, undo the buttons, thread in my arms and walk to the window for another look at the morning as I do it up. Yes, it all looks good. The last button goes in and I walk back for the rest of my clothes. Trousers on over pants, socks and shoes. Now for breakfast on the roof garden.

I go down the three steps quietly so as not to wake the others. The smell of bacon and sausages wafts from the outside kitchen. I go to the small fridge in the lounge that is fitted into the wall next to my cocktail cabinet and open its click door. The jug of orange juice from fruit grown at the big citrus estate outside of Salisbury is frosted white. I take a crystal pint glass from the cabinet, fill it with the fresh orange juice that Kango crushed last night, slam the fridge door, sip and take it out into the new morning. It is fully light and the sky is blooded over a vast area both in itself and in reflection. The high-lying flat clouds are black-shadowed, sombre flecks against the red glow of the central fireball. 'Cheers' to the sun in orange juice. I walk around and up the steps to my roof garden, letting the dewed bougainvillea touch my arms on both sides. I take the last four steps in one pull and here it all is – the whole world for me.

I call down to Kango to serve breakfast.

I wait with the smell of sausages and bacon still wafting to me on the soft new wind. The first cries of the birds, big and small, join the morning. Now the strong aroma of coffee comes up to me here. The chorus of the birds rises sharply as the whole rim of the sun becomes visible. I drink at the cold tang and feel the orange juice going down inside of me. I hear the kitchen door open. I wait, drink the last juice right down, and go over to the small, iron table with its one chair for me and sit. Kango comes barefoot and silently up the iron steps. His head rises first and then the tray. We say nothing. Never do. Smile, yes, and get on with our business. The day has begun.

Fried tomatoes, eggs, sausages, bacon, the small buffalo kidneys, toast, a jug of coffee made from the fresh beans grown outside Umtali, and marmalade. I get hungry in the mornings. He moves away and leaves me to eat. I feed it in quickly.

The first hunger is over with the end of the two eggs under their respective pieces of toast and the sausages. I pour some black coffee, pick up the large cup and slurp at it to get the coffee cool enough for my stomach. I feel its tartness going down with pleasure to make friends with the rest. A piece of buttered toast goes under the tomatoes and off again. The kidneys go into my mouth after the tomatoes and the richness of game satisfies the tail-end of my palate. A piece of toast methodically mops up the gravy and the butter that fired the tomatoes and eggs. I stretch for the toast, the butter and marmalade, put them together and eat. I drink at the cooler coffee, sit back, run a hand through my hair and squint out over the valley and green cane.

The nodding sprays spread a gentle layer of water on intermittent lands. The sky, now colourless, gives a full greenness and natural colour to the earth, hills and valley. The sun shines now and moves its tongue hungrily along, searching out the first flavour of surface dew. It reflects as palest yellow in the cane.

Time I went. I get up, look down on the swimming pool and head for the car.

THE AIRPORT SIGNS draw me and the open-topped Impala through the coloured quarter of Salisbury. I brake and swing and move the heavy car into the short stretches of acceleration, then brake, turn and I have the wide, straight road to the aeroplanes. The needle pushes up to the allowed fifty miles per hour. I sit back with my weight sideways to the wheel. The fast breeze removes the heat from around me. My dark glasses prevent the road glare getting in behind my eyes. I twist my left wrist on the wheel square to myself and glance for the time. Five past ten. I'll have time for a coffee before G5 gets in. I ease off the accelerator and the needle slides back to fifty miles per hour. The engine in front is powerful and easily excited.

I must get them to lay out an airfield on the estate and take some flying lessons to get back my licence. It needs five flying hours a year to keep a licence current. I push my dark glasses onto the bridge of my nose and look up at the blue sky, tinted to brown through the lenses, with firm, well-built clouds that seem to live up there in their own worlds. I must keep Max up to spending his eleven thousand, five hundred pounds on an aircraft. A dozen landings and take-offs with plenty of map reading should get me back my private licence.

I must have averaged sixty-eight miles per hour judging by the milometer and the time. It's a good road all the way except for the turns in and around the coloured quarter. They're building a new road to get over that. The place looks prosperous to me. You don't see Africans with tattered shirts and shorts anymore. There's an air of progress and need to get on. I notice these things as I don't often drive into town. The Africans are independent and wouldn't get off the pavement for anyone. They used to do that in the early days. No, things are looking up all over the country. It's the kind of place that relies on itself and no one else. The outsiders will have a hard job changing any of this. It's too strong and established and there's too much to do to worry about what others think of us. The government we have works well for everyone.

This should be enough for any country. Better than pending economic disaster, the Ku Klux Klan or personal dictatorship. Yes, we've got it all but we mustn't be complacent. So many countries become this when things are going well. Max was right. It is necessary to do something for the whole country, even if it is growing sugar. Exports must remain way above imports. This isn't materialism but a means of self-preservation in the modern world. I can hold the sugar estate as it is if the economy of the country is sound. A strong economy cannot be boycotted or intimidated by countries and people who mean well but haven't quite mastered the facts. They think they have done right by giving freedom to Ghana, Kenya and the Congo. No 'freedom' in Africa has put more food into the bellies of ordinary people. All have put less. Political freedom is a powerful thing to have in our lives. It makes us feel important and in control of our destinies – we are not held down by anyone, we are free. And freedom is the goal of every country as well as every individual. But freedom is a new thing in the 'free' world. Women took political freedom in Britain barely forty years ago and now, so little time later, the cry of universal franchise is heard in the bush and veld and jungle of Africa. Now this is good if the product of universal franchise can provide the basic necessities of human life, but a starving free man is no good to anyone, including himself. It is necessary to glance forward from the immediate freedom and see what it gives in practice, what it gives to all the people and not to a few bureaucrats who channel a large percentage of the small national income into their own pockets. A moral man believes in what is right. Freedom for all the people is right but not if it leads them into starvation, privation and hopelessness of body, which then seeps into the mind and rots the greatest of freedoms. Life is not sustained by freedom but by the work that goes into producing food and shelter, whether directly or otherwise. The luxuries come after, a long time after, and once politics interferes with economics they go more quickly than they come. So, we keep to ourselves here and do what we think is right and are prepared to face our judgement if we are wrong. If you love a country, you have this sense of determination.

The needle is on sixty-four. I shake my head, smile at myself and ease down.

I drop back to thirty miles per hour through the shopping centre, as the sign says I should, and roll to a halt at the red light hanging over the intersection on thick wires. Amber now... To green, and my left foot eases off the clutch pedal as my right pushes down the accelerator.

The car powers itself up and over a short hill and shows me the hangars. Big signs on the closed-in hangar ends tell me the names of international airlines and local charter companies. I slow behind the traffic that is turning into the airport. My turn comes and I swing in right and ride smoothly towards the big cantilevered canopies and long steps that lead up between fluted pillars before flattening out to go into the building. I slide in right again to the car park, find myself a good length of free space, shut off the engine, sit back and clean my dark glasses with a handkerchief, take out the keys, unlatch the door and climb out. I slam the door without looking back and walk down the line of cars towards the main entrance of the airport.

"Air Rhodesia announce the arrival of their flight 113 from Victoria Falls. Air Rhodesia announce the arrival of flight 113 from Victoria Falls. Thank you."

I look around inside. People cross from Red Routes to Blue Routes, in front and behind pillars. Young, blue-uniformed girls with different badges move efficiently from weigh bays to information desks and always across the main, high-roofed, pillar-supported hallway. Old people stand impatiently while others wait with their youth and expectancy. The bustle is constant.

"Will Mr. J. Clack, a passenger from Nairobi, please call at the information bureau. Mr. J. Clack to the information bureau in the main hall. Thank you."

He's probably got an out of date inoculation for something and they're going to send him back. No, Nairobi no longer has its appeal. People look at me. I look around but can't find anyone else in a short-sleeved shirt. Well, how was I to know I should be wearing a shirt and tie? Ten-twenty. Ten minutes for a coffee. I walk across the square-tiled, black and white floored hall and go up in the lift to the first floor and the balcony lounge. I'll be able to see them come in, not that I know what either of them look like but it won't be difficult to pick out a couple of adolescents walking uncomfortably across the tarmac with too many bags, and raincoats. There'll be plenty of time to get downstairs again before they pass through immigration and customs.

I pay the required shilling, go through the turnstile and follow the signs that lead me through the balcony and railings. I look out over the tarmac. The international airlines are usually on time. If it isn't here by ten-thirty-five I'll go down and ask if it's been delayed.

"Waiter, bring me a pot of coffee, please."

"Yes, sir."

I walk a little back from the railings and sit on one of the four empty chairs around a metal-topped table, painted green, that wobbles. I push it around and get all its feet on the concrete. I sit back and relax. There are two aircraft parked on the tarmac. The one furthest away is a new type I don't know with a cocked tail and sharp, hooked nose. The other, nearer, is a Dutch-made twin-engined Fokker Friendship, with Mozambique Airlines printed on its belly. The crew are getting out behind their Portuguese passengers.

A girl of twenty-two, maybe more, four tables away is staring at me, so I take off my dark glasses and stare back, which makes her look away hurriedly and me feel something of a righteous fool. I am used to manoeuvring in the half-light without anyone visibly showing their intentions. If she stared like that on the sugar estate, and happened to be married, the older wives would talk about it for weeks. She looks up again so I wink and she smiles and makes us feel much better as my coffee arrives. She is pretty but draws only superficial interest from me. I pour my coffee, put in half of a small teaspoonful of sugar, slurp at it, remember where I am, and put it down to cool by itself. She is laughing. I put on my dark glasses and stare fixedly out over the Friendship into the heat haze on the other side of the airfield.

It is hot after the car. The heat reflects from the apron below. The other men waiting for the planes are dressed in dark suits – businessmen – the world of commerce, the world I was educated to be part of but went away from – and I have never had the desire to go back to again. I hope they enjoy their lives. We each find our own solution if there is one. I stretch for the small teaspoon and grip it heavily and stir. I clunk it back into the saucer, pick up the cup and drink more in keeping with my surroundings. Another group have sat down between me and the girl. I search the sky for an aircraft.

They could be flying in now. The air is still and heat-sprung, the few clouds motionless. The other aircraft is being obediently towed away, nose first, by a tractor no bigger than its cockpit. More people come onto the balcony. A small boy climbs the first rung of the safety railing in front of me and is hurriedly slapped down by his mother. She looks too old to be his mother. The small boy looks at me for sympathy. I smile him some encouragement. His mouther scowls at me and hurries the little boy away from a bad influence into the lounge. He looks back hopefully over his shoulder as the other is lugged through the open door of the glass-fronted lounge.

It will get hotter but not as hot as in the valley. The river seems far away, as do the buffalo, and yet I left them this morning. I think my father is growing bored but he won't say so for Gwen's sake. She could make a home for herself in this country and be happy with the life. I don't know any bachelors for her but even then their intentions are usually more immediate and satisfying. Women never allow themselves to realise that men are only after this. How many marriages would there be without sex? The attraction is not marital bliss but animal satisfaction and this doesn't need any ceremonies. I must go and tell this to the girl on the fourth table away. Underneath, she probably feels the same as me but, oh, how different it is to 'feel' instead of completing the act that is in our minds. I have acted so on the sugar estate but this is a wild place. The example of conformity isn't there and in its stead is something more basic... And more real. We humans have come a long, strange way. How often do we look at ourselves as animals? Maybe too little.

"British United Airways announce the arrival of their flight G5 from Johannesburg. British United Airways announce the arrival of flight G5 from Johannesburg."

They always repeat themselves! I like the girl's voice so I don't mind listening.

There it is – low and small, far over above the end of the runway. I take off my dark glasses to see better. It grows bigger – still without noise – a new VC10 with the high tail above the dart wings. The jet-roar comes onto the balcony. I can see the four jets now, slung close together in a battery under the tail. The plane drops swiftly. It merges with the ground and bumps on the runway, flashes a dust cloud as it goes up and now down again to settle smoothly and easily onto the earth. It runs swiftly along the tarmac and comes in line with the balcony, its engines roaring to bring it to a halt before it goes off the end of the runway into the bush. Its brakes slow it and bring the forward momentum under control. It trickles to a stop, slews round and with its great mouth pointing up at us comes towards the apron below the observation balcony. A tractor pushing BUA flight steps goes out to meet it at its point of disembarkation. A fuel tanker in bright yellow colours and CAA on its side goes after the ladder lifter. The chipped wing of Central African Airways is more familiar to me than the Air Rhodesia on the tractor. CAA was formed with the old Federation and lost all its planes when it died. The plane turns to give its exit door to our side. The engines roar into my ears. Every particle of eardrum vibrates. The engines cut and my ears hum their way back to normal.

The doors opens in the aircraft sides. The ladders move forward and fit exactly into place. I get up and go to the railings. Others follow from the tables. I put on my dark glasses to counter the tarmac glare and wait for my charges to get out. An air hostess comes out of the hatch first and stands on the landing at the top of the flight of steps. Her right hand goes into the aircraft and the bent form of an old lady comes out. The air hostess doesn't turn to us for applause but helps out another passenger while the old lady shakes the steps in her effort to wobble down to the deck. A ground hostess at the bottom gracefully takes her elbow and guides the old, bent lady to the exit gate down below me. They pass slowly underneath into the building. My eyes go back to the hatch and stop there. A woman is poised to go down the steps, one leg out with complete assurance. She steps down. The ladder remains firm. She looks at her high-heeled shoes until she reaches the bottom and then looks up and across at the balcony. A man in a light-blue blazer moves down next, quickly and efficiently. He catches her up and they walk in side by side. Their movements go easily together. I envy him his youth. She is slightly the shorter in her high heels. Surprisingly, as she walks closer, the impact of grace is enhanced by a long, smooth-skinned face and little or no make-up. Her eyes are behind dark glasses. Her shoulder-length sun-ripe hair bounces gently with her movement – the bottom three inches curl and uncurl with the motion. She carries a small bag and in the same hand a flimsy silk scarf. I've missed something here. I had the buffalo first at his age but I didn't see anything like her in the bush. She looks up as she reaches the railed-off enclosure and shows me the full oval of her face. I study it carefully. I look away, as she disappears underneath, to see if the girls have come off the plane.

The glare is strong even through my dark glasses. Still no young girls in pairs. Nothing at all, in fact, in their late teens. This was G5. Yes, the girl said it twice. The outflow of passengers runs to a trickle and stops. I wait. I look back along the walking passengers, shrug my shoulders and go back to my table. What a long way to come for a cup of coffee. It's unlike Max to make a mistake. Or did he say G5? Yes, he must have done. I was waiting for that number on the Tannoy and heard it twice. They must have got off at Johannesburg and gone their own ways as Max said they would if they were given the chance. These teenagers have no idea of responsibility. They probably wouldn't have minded my driving a thousand miles to meet the plane. The laugh's on Max. He can't blame me for anything that happens in the Republic. I'll have myself another cup of coffee even though it's weak and not as good as Kango's. How's that for the ramblings of a confirmed bachelor? In Europe I'd have a housekeeper instead of a gun bearer to make my coffee but that's the only difference. Half a small teaspoon of sugar and stir well. Most of the people are leaving the balcony. My friend four tables away has gone like so many other people that come and go quickly out of my life. People have gone into the bar that must have opened behind my back while I was watching the aeroplanes. If the girl had stayed I could have taken her for a drive. What else is there to do? I always get bored in town. There are too many things to distract me and unsettle my equilibrium. I could go and see Doris Whitman but she wouldn't be free till this evening. To drive straight back will glue my pants permanently to the seat of the Chev. The bar! The answer to all men's problems when bored or in a quandary. I drink the coffee, slide the chair back and get up. I give the waiter half a crown as I pass him on my way through to the swing doors and the bar. Selling coffee without collecting the price won't make him rich!

"Excuse me, aren't you Mr. Guido Martelli from Gokwe Sugar Estate?"

"Sorry, old man, wrong chap. I'm Mark Harrogate just out from London. Frightfully nice place you have here."

"Sure. Yes, man, I'm sorry I got the wrong bloke. You look a bit tanned coming straight from London."

"Skiing, old boy. Sunglare and all that, gets me very brown."

"Never tried the sport. Don't particularly fancy it either. Enjoy your trip."

He's a salesman who comes up to the estate to sell us an additive oil for the big engines. The oil is very expensive and I'm not yet convinced of its worth and don't wish to talk about it at this stage. He met me in the club bar and, being a good salesman, has a memory for faces that may do him some good.

"A cold Lion lager please, barman."

I've gone off Castle beer. Even though it's the same brewer, I find the Lion more mature and less acidic. It's best to keep it in the fridge for a couple of weeks but they rarely last that long in this heat. The consumption of beer last year in the club worked out at four pints of beer per day per man, woman and child and there are a lot of children. I take the big, thick glass and pour the beer down its side. I drink and let it guzzle down my throat. The time sinks with my beer and I order a second.

"Will Mr. Guido Martelli please go to the reception desk in the main hall. Mr Guido Martelli to the reception desk."

"Cancel that one. Someone wants me."

"I thought you said your name was Mark Harrogate?"

"It is. You ask Max Rosher. And it's also Guido Martelli. I'll let you know when I get the engineer's report. We're testing your oil in all the engines and it takes time."

"Thanks, Mr. Martelli."

"Pleasure. Excuse me now."

"You don't quite fit into the part of an Englishman, if you don't mind my saying so."

"No, that's what I told my father the day before yesterday."

I walk out and along the corridor and turn down the stairs instead of taking the lift.

They can't leave the damn managing director alone and even have to phone two hundred miles for something I can't help with till I get back. Sometimes I'm even more sure that Max can keep his job. I walk from the stairs across the main hall, avoiding people going against my line of travel, to the reception desk. My 'Miss Elegant, Miss Youth and Miss Beauty' is standing by the exit to Red Route with her boyfriend. I have other things to do than concentrate on them. She may be perfect to look at, and better and better as I walk closer to the reception desk, but this is not my problem but the bloke's in the blazer. The badge says 'Rhodesia

Hockey'. He looked that way inclined coming across the apron. Must have played in Tokyo. Well, people like that go together. I'll have to become a big game hunter to get that kind of attention. Now there's an idea!

"My name's Martelli, Guido Martelli. You asked for me over the Tannoy."

"Ah, yes. You're meeting a Miss Maralene Rosher from Geneva?"

"Yes, but she wasn't on the plane. You have a message?"

"No, not at all. She's the girl over there on her own."

"Thanks. She's a co-director's daughter and we haven't met before."

She looks more like twenty-five than nineteen, and more sophisticated than Gwen with all her degrees – a short girl with a thin, well-made figure. I walk across and take off my dark glasses.

"They say at reception you're Maralene Rosher. I'm Guido Martelli. I see your friend didn't come. Where are your bags?"

"Hello. How nice of you to pick us up. Berna met a hockey player on the plane, so I've left them alone for a moment. If we wait here they'll come across. My baggage comes out over there by the main doors but I doubt if it will be ready for a few more minutes. Daddy sent his regards."

"He phoned me yesterday. He wants you both to stay on the sugar estate until he gets back."

"Daddy always thinks of everything."

Yes, she's right, he does. We wait as my eyes go back to the hockey player and Berna. Stella would laugh at me. 'Far too young, my boy, you're past that age group, way past it.'

"We'll go and look for your luggage. Ask your friend to follow us across when she's ready. I'd like to get back on the road as soon as possible now you're here. I have some friends from England staying with me. I left them alone to come into town."

"I'm sorry if we've been a nuisance. We could easily have stayed in town but you know what parents are."

"Fortunately I've forgotten – from both directions. Did you have a good flight?"

"It was more interesting for Berna than me but she found him first."

"I noticed he has played hockey for Rhodesia."

"Yes, he played in the Olympics. They didn't do very well, so he said, but it's quite something to get through the preliminary rounds. He was born here like me."

"Where does Berna come from?"

"Ireland proper. Her father's a landowner in Cork. She doesn't believe we grow sugar in five-thousand-acre lots so I'm looking forward to showing her. Her father has something over two hundred acres, which is an awful lot in Europe. Here, the tobacco farms go around twice that size. There's one of my cases... And there's the other. I think one of those is Berna's. Yes... Thanks... And that one."

"The one next is mine... There."

"This is Berna Larrett. Mr. Guido Martelli."

"Hello. Nice of you to meet us. Yes... And that one. There we are. All together in one piece. This is John Garrup, Mr. Martelli."

"How do you do, sir?"

One says Mr. and the other says 'sir'. How the hell old do I look? I've been in the sun a long time but I haven't withered that much.

"John's been looking after us on the plane."

"It was kind of you, John."

"A pleasure."

I'm damn sure I would have found it one if I'd been your age and just played in the Olympics. It's a sign of age when one envies youth. Some women like older men. But I'm nearly twice her age. Shut up, Martelli, you're even thinking rubbish and that's the best way to start talking it.

"I'll help you put their luggage in your car."

"Thanks, it's just outside."

We walk across in the searing light of the almost midday. The big car reflects the sun sharply from its chrome and I'm glad of it suddenly. It has an importance in context with the one walking beside me with the red silk scarf trailing from her fingertips.

"Which is yours?"

"The one with the hood down."

"You must have a good job to run that. She's beautiful."

"Yes, I make a few pounds when Maralene's father lets me."

"He runs Gokwe Estates."

"You don't seem old enough for a job that big."

"Thanks, John. I'm feeling younger by the day. Put the luggage in here. The Yanks know how to build a car boot."

"Shall we all get in the front?"

"If you like, Berna."

"I'll phone you when Maralene's father brings us into town."

"I'll look forward to that."

"Bye."

"Bye, John."

"See you."

The engine starts smoothly. I fit in the gear and we move forward easily and turn down the line of cars, bear over to the left and turn right onto the main road. Her hip is touching mine and she knows it. How do they find out the tension of men so young? I accelerate quickly up to fifty miles per hour. I relax sideways into my normal driving position and smile to myself – the expression shows in my eyes only and is hidden behind the dark glasses.

"In front is the capital city, Berna. The cluster of skyscrapers is Salisbury. For most of the year it looks like that with the sun in its face and a blue sky at its back. The monstrosity on the immediate left is a cement factory. I don't come often enough to keep pace with the rest of the places that go up."

"Don't you like the nightlife?"

"No, not really. I don't get much enjoyment out of it."

"It depends who you're with."

"True, but putting all the chances together with a drive of two hundred miles is not good enough odds."

"I can never get too much of nightclubs. I've seen plenty in Geneva in the last few weeks. Father also has a house in Dublin and I've seen life in the lights from there. I like to have lots of people around me."

"You sound like someone else I know."

"And what's her name?"

"Doris. Not that the name makes any difference."

"Oh, but it does. I can sum up Doris in that one word."

"You must be very clever, Berna."

"Oh, but I am! Do you mind if I take off the top of this suit? I'm sure the blouse underneath will be enough. If you both lean away from me I'll have enough room."

I begin to swing the car through the coloured quarter.

"That's better. Now the breeze can get at me. I'll tie the scarf around my hair so we can really go fast. I like these cars. They look something, don't they?"

We go through the town at a slow speed that makes me think I can open the door and get out without hurting myself. People stare when we stop at the traffic lights. The speed limit goes up to forty miles per hour. The road curves and the houses thin out and give way to open farmland on both sides. I accelerate and the power pushes us back into our seats.

There is one right turn way up ahead, into the sugar estate, but nothing else.

"My, you sure have plenty of land in this country. Most of it looks as if it hasn't been used. How fast can she go?"

"Over a hundred but it isn't safe at that speed. The road isn't fenced. If some of those cattle over there decide the grass looks better on the other side of the road they just walk across. At seventy-five miles per hour I can stop for most things. At ninety I'm going too fast. I like to cruise at seventy so I get to the other end quickly enough with energy to spare."

"Maralene said you're not married. Seems strange in a man like you."

"I was, Berna, but it didn't last long."

"What went wrong?"

"After six months we didn't like each other."

"There can't be anything simpler than that."

"And you, how many times have you been married?"

"I haven't even thought about the first time. I've been in love but that's different. They say it's much easier to fall in love than get married."

"Not at my age, Berna. I might find it easy to marry someone with mercenary tendencies but this falling in love is more difficult. I have my doubts as to whether it exists – I think it may for other people but that's as far as I've taken it."

The silence lengthens and lets us go into our separate thoughts. What are they thinking? Hockey players, Geneva, parties in Dublin? How nice to be young and look forward with confidence. No, they have their disillusionment to come. I know how much enjoyment to expect.

I haven't been out with a gun for five days. All these people! Next we'll need a hotel on the estate. Gwen ought to stay and see something of the country. These girls may be younger but I have a feeling they've seen more of life than Gwen. When Max gets back he'll bring with him the sophisticated brilliance that I don't have. I should have asked the hockey player to join us. He'd have filled in the time I haven't got to spare. I haven't checked the cane cutting for a week and when I don't, the standard drops. The plant must be pushed to get that extra three per cent through the mill. I put my left arm along the back of the seat. She rests her head back so my arm fits into her neck. We drive on together comfortably, the hot sun burning into my face and the wind cooling it as we cut the warm air. I glance sideways – her face is reddening with the sun. Her eyes are closed and her throat is naked and vulnerable. Without moving my body, I put my hand and wrist through the wheel and press a button while I steer with my elbow. A shadow moves over my head and the hood fixes firmly into the curved and tinted windscreen. The sides remain open. The sun bites my right arm as it goes back to comfortably rest halfway out of the window. If I press the button below my right shoulder, the window will go up too.

"Thanks."

I glance but her eyes haven't opened. I check the road and glance back to look, with surprise, into her open eyes that watch me under the slant of her dark glasses. She smiles softly. I smile back and return to looking at the road. The road goes on straight and symmetrically through the dry bush. The sun burns down on the fast-moving car. We drive on, conscious of each other for a moment, and for a moment, maybe, think ourselves forward into a future circumstance together – and then the threads of other thoughts drift in and take us away to worry or hanker at will.

I BEGIN TO SLOW. Up ahead I can see the hotel turnoff. Just before the hotel is the turn to Kariba. Berna wakes with the deceleration and puts her hand out to the dashboard and pulls herself up. She presses her skirt down to below her knees. Her watch says one-fifteen.

"Are you hungry?"

"I don't know yet. It takes me time to wake up."

"How about you, Maralene?"

"There's a swimming pool here. I'll be hungry after a swim. You can wear your new costume, Berna."

I point the car up the hill at the hotel and climb in first gear. We come out onto the flat carpark below the hotel steps. There is one other car in the carpark. I cut the engine and the heat and silence fold over us.

"I think I'd like to go to sleep again."

Her mouth is softer now that some of the lipstick has been eaten away. The sensual, red skin pushes her lips to join the thicker skin of her face. She lies back against the seat and breathes in heavily and sensually and the rounds of her bra-protected breasts show under the white silk of her blouse. A cat would curl up.

I get out of the car, open the rear door and pull out the cases they ask for. I go round the other side and open the front door. Maralene gets out and stretches. With one case in each hand I walk away to the steps. I look up at the hotel that is looking out to the valley. There are no clouds in the sky, only blueness. I climb the steps one at a time. At the top I look back at the girls. Halfway they stop and look up at me. Berna suggests a shrug directed at the climb and the heat. I turn and go across the flagstones to below the stoep, walk up the four steps and go over to a veranda table and put down the red leather cases. I walk to the flowerbeds in the veranda wall and look out and down onto the blue clear water of the pool.

"If I have the energy to change, it should be lovely in the pool. How do you get it so hot in this country?"

"The sun mainly. It's hotter in the valley. You can change through there. I'll order lunch and we'll eat when you've swum."

"Aren't you coming in?"

"I haven't a costume but I don't need reviving – I'm used to the heat."

"You must have been around here a long time."

They go off with a case each. I signal a waiter.

"Three shandies please and float some ice in them."

The air is invigorating despite the heat. The valley is humid and only cooler by the river. Down there to my left in the heat haze is the distant valley and somewhere in its centre the river. In front, much closer, water bubbles out of the fountain above the filter plant and smoothly slides down to the pool. No one is swimming.

The glasses are heavily frosted and the ice chinks into the still day as the waiter and the silver drinks tray comes nearer. He puts them down one by one and gives me the ticket. I pay him exactly, with a tip, and he goes away in his rubber and canvas shoes with his long, white trousers rubbing each other an inch above the smooth blackness of the floor. He stops with his back to me and looks over the Chev into the distance and hills that hide the Lake Kariba. He has an easy job in the weekdays.

The metal handle to the changing room clicks, the door opens and Maralene comes out into the sun in a one-piece, pale-green bathing suit that shows she has a better figure than her clothes suggested. Her hands hold a handbag, and a towel in the bathing suit colour. She has a small, diamond face with a little chin that pertly finishes the lower contours of her face. Her complexion is pale, like her eyes. Her sales talk is youth in a bathing costume.

"Have a cool drink first."

"Thanks. That looks just divine… And tastes…. It's nice to be back in Africa."

Berna glides herself and a two-piece into the sun. She has piled up her hair to show a long neck that gives the effect of her face being forward and eager. Her middle body moulds in strongly and the curve is centred by a hard, large naval. Her legs are long and in exact proportion to her body. She clicks towards us in high heels that harden and shape the calves of her legs. She moves in perfect balance. Even through our dark glasses she knows I am watching her. She sits next to Maralene and takes up her glass, smiling at me as it gets to her lips. She hasn't made up her face.

"You live well out here, Guido."

She smiles again with my name and I tilt-bow my head to her over my glasses. She lets her tongue run over her lips, with the glass a few inches from her face, and drinks again. Maralene catches our glance, recognises it, but says nothing.

"Are you girls going to swim? How about some chicken and salad for when you come back? We can eat it out here and then you won't have to change. An avocado to start with?"

"We'll leave it up to you."

They get up. Berna reaches the pool and lets herself down into the water. Maralene dives and comes up with hair streaming down her face. Berna swims out gently, keeping her chin from the wet. I signal the waiter and write down the order. He leaves me alone on the stoep to listen to the splashes and quiet small talk of the two in the pool. She is a film in herself to watch. She is soft and pliable to her surroundings and hasn't been changed, yet, by a surfeit of the life she looks for. I drink and watch, and feel the effort of driving go out of me. I stretch my legs hard, side-by-side together under the table. It would be nice to have a bathing costume and go down to the pool. I will swim at home after I leave them with Stella and Jim. He may even change his direction from Gwen with these two in his house. He will like Berna, she is his type. He likes youth as well as maturity so her age won't matter to him. He should have a good two weeks, should Jim. And he won't be able to do a damn thing about it with both of them under the care of Max and one his daughter to report back any troubles. Poor Jim. I'll find it sad watching him! I get up and walk down to the car. I lean in and open the glove compartment and get out a packet of thirty First Lord and a lighter and go back up the steps two at a time. They are getting out of the water and the waiter is laying out avocados stuffed with prawns. The chicken salads are on another table.

"I'd love a cigarette. They seem to have more taste after a swim."

Maralene declines and I offer a light to Berna. She takes the light easily and sits down with the first draw pulled satisfactorily into her lungs. The nape of her neck is wet to a few inches above her hairline. Along her shoulders, large water drops stand out on the deep richness of the skin. We watch each other as we smoke. Maralene begins her avocado. I drink the last of my shandy that won't make me sleep in the heat of the last sixty miles, put my still-burning cigarette onto a square glass ashtray marked 'Castle Beer' on the table away from us, and begin on the food. She throws her cigarette into the flowerbed and turns her attention to food. They talk between themselves but I have nothing to add so I listen. I move the chicken salad in front of Maralene and put the shell of the avocado onto the other table. Berna eats the food with suspicion. Avocado is an acquired taste. She falters so I stretch out for her plate – she lets me replace it with the chicken salad. As I turn for my own our legs touch under the table. They stay that way and I wonder if it matters my being nearly twice her age playing footsy! Ridiculous really. I gently take my foot away to myself and concentrate on the food. Next thing I'll find myself holding Stella's hand! Youth is contagious. I have to drift down to their number of years to find a meeting place – two hundred miles is a long way to come as a chauffeur. Her leg touches mine. There isn't any space left to reverse in. Her sophistication is a veneer and goes no deeper than footsy footsy. I miss this newness in life. It's why I envied her with the hockey player. It 'all' hasn't happened to them before. Each stage will be exciting – even the ending for him. He'll live in hope, at the age of twenty-one, of her phoning. Maybe she will. Maybe they'll even get married and live happily ever after and prove me, the cynic, hopelessly wrong. I hope so but I doubt it. Life isn't perfect like her face is in this youth. And even if a patch of life is good it won't stay that way, and neither will her face when she gets older. But I enjoy it for now and have no concern about what happens tomorrow. But just maybe she has, and this is her trap and unhappiness to come and it may not come through me. She may find that what she feels now isn't there – as it isn't really. This moment has no true relevance or consequence for any future in minutes, hours or years.

The heat and food together with my emotions close in around me tightly. My mind thinks within my skull and the thoughts go round and round. Time holds itself still. I eat and drink and bend towards my plate.

I sit back and look up to see how far the sun has gone over and check the mental estimate with my watch. Four minutes out.

"Shall we go when you're ready?"

"Our costumes have dried so let's go and change."

They get up and walk away to the changing rooms. I watch them go, then take another cigarette out of the packet – reflex action – too much looking is bad. I flick the lighter and let the smoke drift out of my mouth and watch it drift above my eyes. A hawk circles the sky and glides away behind the roof.

THE CLICK, click and they're coming my way again. Berna's blouse is open over her costume. Maralene has on soft, elfin-toed shoes that fight the contrast of her thighs – and that's it with the costume.

"Ready? Do you mind if we go like this?"

"Have you got something to put on over your shoulders when we get to the estate? My labour would talk about it for weeks otherwise."

"I can use the towel."

"That'll do. Let me take the cases. Sure you've got what you brought?"

"You think of everything."

"Age does that."

"You're not so much older than us."

I let them go first down the steps – there isn't room for the three of us side by side with the bags. I look out over the hills towards Kariba instead of at the rear and rhythmic movement of Berna. They walk to the car. She gets in from my side and slides across. I put the cases in the back, hold the door for Maralene, shut it firmly, go round the front of the car, duck down and get in behind the wheel. I put the steering wheel lever into reverse, tread down the clutch and start the car. The reverse engages easily. We go back, swing round and stop before going forward down the hill. We turn left onto the tarmac. The road will drop slightly before we reach the escarpment. The winding begins and the heat increases. In front is the heat-soaked valley, flat and motionless.

We ride down and come out onto a straight road.

The first road sign warning us of elephant comes up on our left and flashes past. I drive with my right hand and let the left go down to rest on the seat. I feel her hand move into mine. Her skin is soft. The gnarled, heavy bush of the valley and the strong, heat-pressed smell of animal and vegetation goes by on either side. My nostrils pull in the varying smells of the air layers we pass through. I scan each new waterhole for duck or game. The now flooded pits were originally dug by the road makers to level the scar they were trying to perpetuate. The animals made them part of the bush but still have no use for the road. I glance sideways at her. Her head is back. I swallow. I haven't felt like this since I was young. I look at women and still feel the signal but experience puts down my excitement and tells me the body will be the same as the rest – nothing new. I feel her eyes compelling me to turn. She smiles. I smile too and tell my emotional self that she is like the others, young, yes, for my vanity, but the same to be got used to and satisfied by – for a while or a little longer. Her skin is very pure. I look at my hand on the wheel and tell it to tell the other to grow up. But it doesn't. Maybe there is a spirit in me that has never been satisfied and never grown up. Maybe this part of me joins with her youth and produces the sense of feeling that never lived before because I never meet what I have met now. Have I been wrong about women? This is how it should be – a natural impulse not directed by pre-thought or post-thought. It could be that this happens with the same rarity as brilliance or it could be that it will go as fast as it came and become a skeleton of my past with no flesh, just the dry, stark memory to show that these things are not really alive. I put my left hand back on the wheel, straighten my arms and press my shoulders hard into the seat to squash myself back to normality. The road is hard, straight and miraged in front by heatwaves. Imaginary water shimmers for me and stays in the distance. A squat, ten-mile peg, with the miles in black on white, comes up quickly and goes by even faster. I ease off the speed and the road shrinks into us. I laugh inwardly at myself and feel better.

A warthog is drinking by itself on the far side of the waterhole over there. It takes no notice. Alone, I would brake firmly, stop, reverse back, get the gun out from under the rear seat – specially hollowed so the game rangers don't know it is there and in particular Ted, who knows I poach even as the boss – and shoot out across the water from the car.

I brake slowly and pull the other foot off the accelerator. I swing the car in right onto the gravel road and the pound of wheels on rutted molasses jerks my sense rhythmically into satisfaction.

The factory chimney comes into view briefly between the trees. I glance in the rear-view mirror at the dust trail. The sun is losing its glare. The road rushes suddenly into green cane. I slow back. Maralene wraps her towel around her shoulders. Berna sits up and looks at the sugar cane. I feel comfortable now I'm back in the valley. I cut back the engine and we rumble past the cane in second gear. Africans wave to us from the tops of the trailers, stacked with bundles of sugar cane that lurch loosely behind their pulling tractors. They laugh easily these people. Three more get off their bicycles before I pass, and pull their machines away from us close into the cane that is dust-coated so near the road. The tussling tops of the sugar cane lean over and make the sky above us smaller than the road under our wheels. I swing the car in past the crushing factory and look quickly down the length of shed as we pass to see if anything is out of place. The machinery is turning and crushing and boiling and crystallising the sugar as usual.

"The smell is overpowering."

"Molasses, Berna. You get used to it and like it eventually."

"It's incredible to find so much greenness after all that dry bush."

"You can see it better from my house. We'll go there first."

## 13

*H*er back is towards me. I walk out from the veranda in my bathing costume. The shape of her body is made tantalising by the sun. My feeling for her now, walking across the harsh kikuyu grass is strong. She turns on her hips to see who it is behind her and the sun delineates the contours of her breasts. Her skin is smooth all over and the smoothness of her two-piece is firm. I stop beside her and look down at our reflections in the pool. In front is the valley and the sun reflecting in the slow, nodding sprays. The escarpment hills are golden.

"I thought you'd gone down to the Marshams with the others."

"I said I wanted to swim instead. In Ireland we don't often see this kind of weather."

"It'll be like this for six months."

"So you tell me."

"If you stay you'll grow used to the sun being up there every day."

I put my hand on the curve of smooth, heavy skin above her furthest hip and feel it gently and run my hand down over the smooth material. I feel up her back and press hard at the nape of her neck, where strings of hair have come loose from a red scarf.

"I feel all peculiar, Guido. I think I'd better get into the water."

"I wish I was ten years younger."

She dives into the water, her hair forgotten. I watch and wear my age with little composure. There are certain things we can't have and this, for me, is one. She doesn't even understand what she is creating in me. Hers is all youth. She still does the natural thing or the one she has just learnt. She doesn't have a textbook of technique in her mind. She has never seen the consequence of herself on someone.

She surfaces, finds her feet a contact with the bottom and pushes her hair and scarf back over her head.

"Why don't you come in?"

I keel over and go down to meet the water and slice it, conscious of my movement as much as I am of her. I try and think down here beneath the water but no intelligence comes to me. I am conscious of something slipping away from me but that is all. I surface and kick over onto my back so there is only me, the water and the sun in my world. How much is wishful thinking? – how much is hope? – how very little is reality? – a holiday for her that should be a job of chaperone for me like looking after a child, the child in my imagination that I didn't conquer when I should have done. Those two years of army gave me something but prevented, through lack of opportunity, this part of my mind maturing and when I did I got straight into bed and left the emotions unchecked.

Water splashes onto my face. I jerk myself round in the water and drop my feet down onto the smooth tiles at the bottom. I splash back and we laugh. I strike out after her and she turns tail. I grab her leg so she flounders. She wriggles hard. I let her go. She swims away on her back and hits the water hard with the palm of her hand. A smooth arc of water spurts towards me. I lurch forward with both hands grasping but she is too quick. She gets away into the shallow end and stands at the bay, defiant, with brown, large eyes looking at me softly, her breasts heaving with her expended effort. The sun and water – together they shine on her flesh. She runs the palms of her hands down from her eyes over her face, squeezing her breasts together with her elbows. I'm glad I'm standing in cold water.

"Why can't we just stay in your house instead of with those people?"

"It wouldn't look right. It's necessary for the boss to conform in a community where we work and live in the same place. In your Europe it's possible to keep one's private life from the people who pay you but not here. You'll like Jim and Stella, but especially Jim. He was a great ladies' man before he married. Still is, I suppose. A family looking after two attractive girls is right. A bachelor is not."

"It seems all right for Gwen."

"That's different. Her father's here."

"But he must sleep sometimes."

"Gwen is different."

"Why? Are you having an affair with her? You seem pretty close to each other."

"What do you know about affairs, Berna? They are usually sordid and end without satisfaction."

"I'm not so inexperienced as you think. I've got you pretty well organised and I only got off the plane six hours ago. No, I like to have fun. It gives life an interest. Unless there's someone around to get off with, life's dull."

"There'll be Jim in the other house."

"He may not like me."

"He will."

"He's married."

"And so was I but just because a magistrate signed some papers it's all right for you to make a pass at me and drag out a response."

"I didn't notice much of a dragging."

"No, you're right. There wasn't any. For just a moment I thought I'd found something I'd lost – my youth. But now I've got all my thirty-five years back again and they fit and once more Guido Martelli is back on his feet. Shall we get out and have a drink? We don't want it to appear as though we've spoiled their matchmaking. My relatives would be most upset."

"How close are they in relation to you?"

"Pretty close, Berna, and they think I'm too old not to be married but I'm convinced they are wrong. I'll race you out of the water to the veranda. If we run hard enough we'll be dry when we get there."

I wade to the side and spring up and twist around to face the water. The tiles are cooler under the lowering sun. I sit with my feet dangling in the water. A lot has come and gone in so short a time. Nothing in human relationships is suddenly there, perfect. And this recommended moulding process is too much a means of destroying what I am inside of me. I can suppress me and teeter along the life of compromise as most others do, but still, deep down in my gut, there will be no peace or rest or satisfaction. What does it matter anyway?

I get up and walk back across the lawn to the house. Alone, I would go out by myself with the gun. The danger there can be seen and understood – there are no words to parry, no intangible blind alleys to stagger along.

I walk through into my bedroom and put on a T-shirt and thong shoes. I look around at the pure, healthy untidiness of bachelorhood and the old, dried skins on the floor and the line of rifles chained to a bracket against the wall. There isn't a touch of woman in this room. Any that come in, come in for my purpose and leave no marks on the furniture. Now for a drink. I feel like a real, good strong drink to bring back the full man in me and remove any feminine chinks. They all have that something different and it's this we're after and nothing else. The rest are trappings so they can force their security on us – a myth that never existed except in the hopeful minds of wishful, lonely men when the things of man don't quite satisfy him and he looks to woman for something else. He doesn't know what it is but makes one hell of a mess searching just the same. Oh, yes, that drink.

I stop looking out of the window, cross to the door, open it and go into the lounge. Ice is already on the cocktail cabinet. Kango never forgets. She's sitting on the veranda with the tail-end of the long, running sun licking over the beauty of her. It's still hot. The humidity is high. I make her a John Collins with gin and lemonade and the herbs and fruit slices left by Kango, pour myself a whisky in a wide, crystal glass on top of five ice rocks and go out to her with the drinks.

"Try this. It may bring us back to normality."

"Do you want to?"

"I think it's wise. Just rest on what I think for once."

"Who else is coming to dinner tonight?"

"The Marshams, a game ranger who always stops from catching me poaching and Gwen and her father. I'm sorry the hockey player couldn't be here. It's unusual to feed more women than men at Gokwe. We'll look around for something tomorrow. There may be the odd American in the valley on a hunting trip. They're usually old and fat but sometimes not."

"I'll be quite happy with you."

THE SPUR-WINGED GOOSE makes good eating – it looks well, steaming among the roast potatoes on its oval plate. I run the razor-sharp knife down its crisp-roasted side without any pressure and the cooked meat folds down from the carcase. The carved slices go one by one onto the plates for Kango to take round to the guests. The chatter of voices mingles with the polished silver and glasses that go right on down the length of the table. If I wasn't a bachelor they might have had candles. I take the last full plate for myself and sit down at the top of the table.

They talk with each other and to each other. Stella throws words across the table at Ted. He replies. What they say is irrelevant and part only of what is expected of them. Are they enjoying themselves? Father is talking down to Maralene and she up to him. She looks her youth tonight. Gwen is on my right and Maralene on the other side. Ted is opposite me, with Stella and Berna on either side of him. We face each other, Ted and I, with the 'poached' goose behind us on the sideboard, ravaged by my knife and drying its carcase bones for all to see. Geese shooting is out of season. I shot it last week while practising with my .22 revolver. It came up over a reed-spiked sand dune with a bend in the river behind. And now here I am feeding cooked bits of it into my stomach. I drink at the wine Father pours for me and the clean, cold tang removes the immediate goose grease. I think that Gwen and Jim Marsham are playing footsy but Stella is too interested in Ted to notice. She has been necessary for me over the last year. We will probably go on serving each other's purposes until one of us finds someone else or Jim takes a shot at me and doesn't miss.

I go back to eating and concentrate on getting the bits of goose, roast potatoes, stuffing, squash and pumpkin into my mouth as quickly as possible. I stop for breath, get it, stretch out for the hock glass and slurp some wine down my throat. I had four mint juleps before I started this little lot. With luck they won't notice my shovelling manners. I am sure Jim and Gwen are rubbing each other. They both have that faraway look of expectancy. At this stage the whole thing is nice for them – very new and interesting.

Back to what's left of the goose on my plate. Now how can Stella get herself alone with Ted tonight? Difficult. And poor Berna isn't getting any attention. I give her an intoxicated grin down the table. I don't think my face expresses the right sentiment. Those big brown eyes are appealing to me. I fill up my glass, and Maralene's and Gwen's on either side, suggestively wag the bottle at Jim to distract him back to the alcohol, succeed, have the bottle taken away from me and my right hand is free to get at my glass. I bring it towards me over the almost empty, greased-up plate surrounded by still gleaming cutlery, and drink. The alcohol is getting hold of my brain. I enjoy the inertia and fug. I don't have to think seriously in this kind of mood. We must find Maralene a boyfriend. But there it is – she'll just have to write off this fortnight as not for her and look forward to something better when she gets off the sugar estate.

One by one the clattering, and sometimes the chattering, stops. Kango removes the immediate debris and brings on a jellied conglomeration in red as a pudding. He and I are good at cooking things like goose but not much else. If it wasn't for the sherry he's sneaked out of my cocktail cabinet and into the red goo it would be repulsive. I look up. Kango is watching me. I very slightly shake my head and he grins. Women's food, this stuff.

I answer their questions with the bottom of my mind while the top floats around up here with the alcohol and a perpetual grin. The world of diners goes on below me, none of my real concern.

I look across. It's completely dark outside. No moon yet. I listen to the cicadas grinding away at their back legs. The frog-croaking noises come in from the pool through the lounge doors. They will be enjoying themselves with all that dark and water. My watch says almost ten o'clock. My mind must have addled while I was thinking, and lost an hour or more. I don't remember that much time going by. Time renews itself without any problem. Time has eternity ahead of it for itself. It cannot be destroyed by age or bombs or illness.

"Shall we have coffee on the veranda? If the mosquitoes are too bad we'll move back into the lounge."

"I enjoyed that, son."

"Not so much of the paternalism or they'll be thinking you're my father and that would spoil my play for Gwen."

"Sorry, I forgot. No, on second thoughts I wouldn't want him as a son."

"You can laugh. Each one of us had a father so it's just a question of pitying mine. After you, Maralene."

"I think the bugs are too much. Look at the praying mantis on the lightshade."

"Horrible and ugly isn't he? And very methodical the way he tears bits off that spider. All right. The ladies win. Draw the screens across the sliding doors, Kango, and turn on the air conditioning. Let's all be civilised. Gwen, will you pour out the coffee? I'll leave the liqueurs to you, Jim. Ted, you know how to work the record player. Put on something gay. I'm sure the girls will appreciate some music. It livens the spirit like the first waves of alcohol."

They sit and Father sprawls and we wait for the interchange of small coffee cups and liqueur glasses. I sit back and watch Kango draw the wire-mesh folding screens. Dark out there. Nothing but black to be seen in the darkness. The door-sized sections of the screen flatten out like unfolded concertinas and shut us away from the big and little bugs. There are eight sections to the shutters. Kango pushes the wooden-framed screen against the one window to my left as I peer out into the darkness and try to make my eyes penetrate the night even though my pupils are shaped for the electric lights in here. When wanted, the screen folds inwards and the window outwards. Both shut, they face each other.

The music goes on. The records belong to the company and are here for such occasions. I never play them myself. If I get bored in the evenings I take the heavy gun and go out with the spotlight strapped to my forehead and the switchgear strapped to my side.

A band on the record produces music in fast time to Berna's right foot. I must have missed a whole generation out here in the bush. We stare at each other. I try to look inside of her and find what is there for me. The wine has silenced us all. The music dominates. The small areas of our eyes search the others. She is underneath the window, in shadow from the three standard lamps around the room. Her eyes are visible in a trick of the light. My legs are stretched in front of me, half towards the pool and half to her. My folded hands rest lightly on the digesting goose. The low coffee table is between us all, nearer to me and towards the middle of the room. There are three Persian rugs on the highly polished smoothness of the slasto floor.

We each have our liquors and coffees now and our private, foodful, drinkful thoughts. My eyes are separate from me and look at Berna. My foot is tapping with hers and not with the music. My eyes look quickly out of the window above and behind Berna and then back at her looking at me. I feel I want her – but for what reason? Is it passion or sympathy? Is it hope or failure? Is it the end of my youth or the first walk of my old age and impotency? Is it just me or a little of both of us? Is it her eyes or... Oh, shut up, Martelli. Your mind is addled with fatigue and too much food. True... True, but I'd still like to know which one it is. What is Stella wanting? Why did she marry Jim? She must have been bored with her foreigner's life in Paris. She never talked of those days to me. I know nothing about her really. And yet we act to perpetuate ourselves in each other. The satisfaction we transact should produce for us children. In animal life this would be so. In human life we divorce these things from each other and try to take them separately. We mate with what we don't know and don't even ask ourselves why. Surely the animals are wholly involved with each other for the moment of fusion, even if afterwards they separate and look for someone else in the next season. But not us. We satiate our bodies and then stretch out for a cigarette immediately afterwards, and having had that feel hungry for food.

Ted committed himself completely to the bush. Maybe I should have done the same. A little of society doesn't have time to destroy his self-respect – it is too soon lost, once again, in the bush. A game warden's life is pure if lonely. But after a long time loneliness is company in itself. He is a whole person by himself. He thinks, whereas he should hope, that she is flirting with him because she finds him attractive, because he is something special – and her husband doesn't even watch, engrossed as he is in his own point of interest. Jim lives for these moments as he likes a change. His sexual solvency can only be found in variety.

Maralene sits back – it isn't her turn to come up on the stage. She must remain bored for the moment – nothing is happening to her.

The air conditioning takes control of the temperature and it slowly drops – mechanical power has defeated the elements – sweat no longer grows from my forehead and the clamminess in my hands recedes. I am left with a clean feeling and Berna watching me. The gauze screen over the window moves. There is no wind. The fug and fuddle in my mind tries to evaporate. I stretch my left leg out to the coffee table and hook my foot around the short, gnarled leg. I seem to be looking over to the left of the window, to above Berna's head. The music is loud. My vision is wide enough to be conscious of her tapping foot. My left foot pulls in and it slowly slides towards me. The screen moves. My leg cramps as I pull. The screen shudders slightly.

"Berna, if you sit over this side you can hear the music better."

"Sounds like an invitation, but I don't mind."

She gets up. The screen shudders harder. A slice of the night appears between the wall and the light's reflection on the mosquito gauze. She brings the wicker chair with her and blocks me from whoever is outside. I pull hard on the table and jerk it in front of me.

"Come on over this side, Berna."

Ted and Stella are quietly talking to each other. Maralene's feet tap out the music. Father seems asleep. Gwen looks at Jim as though she'd prefer us not to be here. The window is half open. It's black out there. I lean my elbows forward on my knees so my hands are free and below the table.

"Berna, lean over to me. I want to whisper something."

"Why don't you lean towards me? I can't do all the chasing. I should have made you cross the floor. Why don't you look at me?"

She leans closer and I smell the youth in her perfume.

"Because someone's watching us from outside. Don't look. Just keep talking to me. I have a gun strapped under this bloody table but if I jerk for it he'll have more time to shoot than me. The screen's moving again."

"Don't be silly. It's the wind. Things like that don't happen."

"This is Africa, Berna, and here they do… and there isn't any wind tonight."

I inch my fingers along the rubber straps and feel the coldness of my .22 revolver. Only Kango may know it is here, having come across it while cleaning. Jim Marsham has no idea it lives under this table to guard against his jealousy. The barrel is towards me. I push the gun against the rubber strap and free the nose from the thong that holds up the barrel. I twist and ease it towards me. The butt comes free and the gun is mine. I turn the barrel to face the wall below the window.

"Get up and go to Jim and Gwen. Tell them quietly to get out of the room and tell Jim to circle the house."

"I'm frightened."

"Do as I say and don't argue. And walk around the back of me."

She gets up. My eyes focus on the gramophone which sits in the alcove beside the fireplace. My width of vision gives me the opening window but no one else has the sense of being watched. Whoever it is is not a hunter – not a professional. A match flares and illuminates an African in the window. The flame licks towards a piece of rag jutting out of an orange juice bottle. The rag leads into a slit in the metal cap. The rag flares and flames engulf the neck of the bottle and tries to get in at the liquid inside. The man's eyes glint in the light he has made. His left hand thrusts at the screen. The other holding the bottle goes up and back above his head. I squeeze the trigger viciously even as I pull the revolver from under the table. The bottle explodes and petrol erupts over his head. He screams – a long animal howl. I vault out of the chair and run into the bedroom, grab at the counterpane and knock into Ted before I burst through the flimsy screen of the folding doors. The walls are flaming with petrol. The stench is petrol and burning flesh. The curtains are alight inside. I hold the counterpane at arm's length and run-thrust at where he is burning just away from the main holocaust. I smother him and the unsuffocated flames creep out from the folds and clutch at my face and tear at my hair. Someone else throws a blanket over him. I hear Jim's voice coming from inside but recognise nothing he says… The two of us roll out the flames. I get up. I look around but the flames on the walls are nearly out and the darkness has crept back again. The gun is still in my right hand and Ted's breathing is heavy beside me.

"He's dead, Guido. Christ, he's dead and it should have been us. What makes a man want to kill like that? Politics? How much rubbish must they have told him to make him act like that? – all the filth – all the bloody hatred. I've seen some shooting, Guido, I've seen some people shoot for their lives before, but my God, I've never seen that speed. I saw that bomb raised above his head. The light caught my eye. He was throwing it then. Your gun came out as his arm went back but you shot it first. We'd have all fried in that confined space. With the impact of the throw, the bomb would have exploded all over the room."

"Are there any more of them, Ted? Go and get my rifle from my gun safe. Here are the keys. Give Jim and Gordon Harrogate one."

"Guido… Guido, the telephone is dead."

I glance inside the window.

"Turn out the lights."

I go back in the house.

The petrol has burnt itself out on the curtains that lie charred and half-suffocated under the carpet. Berna is sobbing. I think it is her. The pelmet still glows.

"Shut up crying. We must think clearly. This one was not from my labour gang. He must have come across the river. No, it can't even be that as my labour would have told me. And if this had been political and he'd come over the river, his friends would have attacked again with machine guns. A single fanatic – maybe that's what he was. The telephone wire goes out above the window and could have been burnt by the petrol. Follow my voice into the bedroom, Ted, and I'll give you the guns. They're over there. Give me back the keys. I know the shape of the lock… A .303 – you know the feel. They're all loaded. A gun is just metal without a bullet in its breech. Stay and look after the women. I'm going to look around. This is my valley. Anyone who wants to throw bombs in it answers to me. Are you sure he was dead?"

"He didn't have any eyes left – they were burnt right out – and the flesh was hanging from his throat. Yes, he was dead. The bomb went off just above his head."

"If I'd shot him, the reflex could have thrown the petrol into the room. Only had time to kill the bomb."

We walk into the big room. The shapes of everyone are visible in the dark. Why didn't he light the taper below the windowsill and make one push at the screen? Fear... Yes, he must have been frightened. Maybe he knew me. Maybe he wanted to be sure that there wasn't a gun within my reach. But he should also have known that my eyes have trained themselves over the last eleven years to focus instantly on movement. But how could he know I fear my girlfriend's husband and keep a gun for him under the table – husbands want to talk first – when they do I intend talking across the coffee table. This was known by me only – maybe also by Kango. What did he die for – or live for? The shock and exploded glass made it instant. The consuming need of flames for more oxygen sucked the air from his lungs and the flash of heat and pain crumpled his life.

I walk out onto the veranda, using my senses to see instead of my eyes.

"Don't go, Guido. I'm frightened."

"It's my job, Berna. I'll be back when I'm sure it's safe. I'm sorry the party came to this. If Kango comes up from the compound, tell him to look for me. Don't turn on the lights until I get back. You're easy targets with the lights on and you can't see what's out in the night."

I go out, cross the lawn and go past the swimming pool and begin to climb down the hill. I loose no stones nor make any noise but hold the gun firmly and accurately in front of me. The cartridges I took from the gun safe are heavy in my pocket.

My eyes are used to the light of the stars. No moon. The hill gives out onto the road and I move across it and walk beside the cane. There is too little light to identify me.

How can this have happened in the valley? If we behave like this the end will come to us as quickly as it will to the buffalo. We will all die and there will be no one to look back on history. Only the river will go on flowing – but by itself – forever – and the rain will fall in the season.

I walk on as part of my own destruction and make no sound – like the crawl of death. Eternity laughs at me – chuckles itself up in its belly at my ridiculous fight. What do the Bernas matter? There is a greater need in me than just for a woman – a need to understand my life – a need to tell myself there is a real purpose, a real need for me being alive. There must be more to us than just each day after day until we die... like him. We are able to understand too much to be snuffed out into charcoaled bones. This ability to be alive cannot be as vulnerable as it is. There must be something definite for us to understand that doesn't have to be supported by the many hopes of many religions.

I go further, holding my gun, my means of destruction and preservation, my answer so far as it will take me to the brink where I will still understand, where my brain will still work and then will go over, sharply, quickly to where there is no coming back and no knowledge or slightest comprehension what is there. Darkness will be me.

Nothing is on both sides of our lives – at the beginning and the end. I have tried in the valley to live my life for what I understand it to be, for what I know of it. And in these years by the river I have been successful. But I am now forced out of my sensibility into the world of reality, into the world of madness, into the harsh consciousness of life's great laugh, its great stupidity for being here at all. There is nothing. That is the joke. The road, the gun and Guido Martelli – but nothing really. Only life, death and the matter that is earth and rock which ignores me, because it has no feeling – no love nor pain nor hunger. This love and feeling is for us – only. But we don't matter. We can come and go as quickly as we like. Even as we try to destroy someone else we become nothing. I can think now because I am alive but he is completely dead and has no ability for anything, not even an ability to realise he is dead. When alive there is only our instinct which forces us to remain so for as long as possible, to survive the others. When dead, even the life didn't exist because whatever did can only have done so through ourselves. If I had no life the world wouldn't exist. If I had not lived there would have been no world.

The road is deserted. There are no fires in the night. The houses on the estate are not burning. Elsewhere there is peace and silence. Here, only, I grip the gun. Up there, only, I preserved my life... and for what? The joke is there, right in front of me. Its humour is sick all over. It vomits up its cackling craziness and truth.

There is nothing above or around me in the night. The animals are either full of food or asleep. I plod the shadows looking for my phantom or maybe my life.

I level my revolver at the stars and pull the trigger harshly till the explosions stop and the hammer hits home at the empty shells. So much for my soft footwork. All right, everyone! I'm here now. Guido Martelli is here and his gun is empty... Nothing happens. Not a thing. I wait. No one comes. I am ignored. The shots were between me and the stars. I am so much nothingness, so much irrelevance to the world.

I keep walking in the night.

THE PATH HAS TURNED and takes me on my way back home. Time has been lost in the movement of my feet. My mind has been thinking spasmodically and now shifts back to normal. It comes back to the feet and the earth. It walks alone but real. It doesn't want to understand. It has no need to go down into the depths of my mind for understanding. It can come back to the feet and the earth and be satisfied for the moment with what I know, with what I understand. The heavens are still above me and the gun is empty. There is no moon. There wasn't that before. There is me. There is no one else trying to kill me. I can tell the others to put on the lights. When I get back I'll go out with Kango and the big guns. Together we understand this part of our seeable, tangible lives. And this is as far as we need to go. The beginning and the end are for the past and the future, the two ends that have never been seen before and never been understood.

## 14

"What are you doing down here, Berna? You were meant to go back with Jim and Stella."

"I couldn't face going out into the dark. I thought you'd be back sooner. I don't feel secure anymore unless you're in the room."

"Where is Father and Gwen?"

"He's upstairs. Yes… I suppose that is it. It tells me a lot about the way you behave with them. Guido, will you hold me? Please squeeze some of the fright out of me. Why didn't they say they were your father and sister? Hold me tighter."

"I changed my name by deed poll eleven years ago. To explain the difference in name and nationality to the whole estate would have taken too long. Are they asleep?"

"Your father is. I like him. He understands a lot more than he says. He didn't even question my wanting to stay here. He asked me to shout if I needed help and left me that gun as protection. I know how to use it. My father taught me to shoot in Ireland when I was twelve – he didn't have a son. Your father took another rifle and went upstairs to sleep. Gwen went off with the other three for a drink. She said she needed one… And people to talk to. She's been a long time. You feel nice against me."

"Do you know what it's all about, Berna? No, you don't, and I wish I was as young as you. If you knew, you'd be frightened of me now. I think we'd better sit down. My nerves are still tense and liable to make me do things I'd regret tomorrow. You see, I don't want you to fall into the same class as Stella, and probably Gwen, especially after this evening is out and Jim has traded on the situation – I think if his tension keeps up from the fire attack he'll forget what Ted's trying to do to his wife. I hope Maralene sees none of it. It's a part of life we all come to and when we do, and take it to excess, it removes our pride."

"But it can be beautiful. Between two people who really love each other there can be nothing more wonderful or clean. It's an expression of beauty in each other. It's the means of expressing what I feel. And tonight I do want to be felt. I used to tease but I'm not anymore. I want you to flood me with yourself as only in this way can I feel safe. No, really Guido, I don't mind what you do with me."

"But I do. If you were just another woman, as I'm trying to think you're not, then I'd educate you in the bedroom. But if I did that I'd do what I want to for the moment and destroy something more valuable for tomorrow. Maybe you don't matter to me but I think you should and if I kill it now there will be nothing for me in the future."

"We'd be much closer. I'm sure you'd mean as much to me if not more. Otherwise you'll have to marry me and then you won't be able to refuse... I don't understand you. All the other men I've known have tried to bed me on the second question. That hockey player was trying to do it on the plane when he thought the others were sleeping. We had seats next to each other. He just wanted sex and the more I pushed him away, the more he wanted me. But you look so lonely at me I just want to cry... And then I want to hold you... And then I want you all over me and I want to be smothered. And now I've got to asking you. It's all wrong and I don't understand."

"Oh, I want you, Berna, but I don't want to destroy you. I want to think of you as different to the others. You're the most attractive woman I've come across, if that means anything to you. To look at, you're perfect. The rest I can only find out about with time. No, if we got married we'd end up hating each other like most married couples. It's not worth the chance."

"Just get me a blanket and I'll go to sleep here on the couch. Everything has gone cold in me. I don't mind if they throw another of those things in the window. I never get anything I want. My life's a frustration in one way or the other and this is the perfect joke at the end. Thanks. No, don't bother. Berna will tuck it in. With your father in the house they shouldn't talk too much so stop frowning about your reputation. I won't dirty the precious name of the Big White Boss. You can go and rest in the sanctity of your bedroom, alone. Maybe there's something wrong with you sexually, and that's why you live by yourself."

"Maybe there is. Maybe there's a whole lot wrong with all of us. I would like to be like other people and hide my life in a marriage and children and all those small things of a home that mean nothing but soak up so much of the time. I only wish I could believe this was the reason for us being alive and that it would satisfy my emotions. Berna, I know what will happen. It'll all come tumbling down like the other progressions in life and then there will be no important stage to look forward to except my death – but I won't be alive at my funeral so I won't be able to judge its success or otherwise. I prefer you to remain as a possible source of stability. I'm too frightened of reality to try and find out. I can't take the chance that you'll become nothing."

"I don't understand what you've said."

"You will... Maybe when you're thirty-five. Maybe the African outside had reached the age of no progression. Kango knew him for three years when he worked with the sugar. And then I had him fired because I thought he didn't work hard enough. Who was I to judge? In his way he probably worked harder than most and tonight's tragedy is that his capacity for work didn't fit into my modern economics. After, when he didn't have a job, and without a tie of family, he didn't have anything to go forward to except his revenge and now the police have his charred remains. The sun's not far from getting up. I'm tired. Exhausted is the better word. I'll see you later in the morning. Try and sleep and everything will find a perspective – even for both of us."

I bend and kiss her firm, young lips and taste the moisture in her mouth. She responds gently. I pull a little away from her face and look down into the softness of her large brown eyes. I touch the smoothness of her skin. Her eyes follow mine as I look round her face.

"I'll turn out the light."

I go round the settee, turn out the standard lamp and find my way from long practice into my bedroom, undress and get in under the sheet and one blanket. This is the coldest time of the night or day – dawn. I've just killed someone and yet I go to sleep as I always do. The pillow is cool. My feet touch the board at the bottom of the bed. I roll over onto my left side.

# PART TWO

### 1964

# 15

Hunched motionless against the driver's door of my Land Rover, I look out over the newly levelled runway. It took two bulldozers ten days to tear up the trees and level the ground. The morning sun presses down on my head and the metal around me is too hot to touch. It's nice to be alone in the early morning, alone and sitting and waiting and not caring whether they come at all – the combined pleasure of solitude and the sun is quite sufficient. What a dust cloud they'll make when they land! To finish the strip we sprayed water on the smashed earth. It hardened the surface but the sun has since scorched up a layer of weightless dust.

My guests are still in their various beds. I should have brought some breakfast. My rifle in its pads this side of the windscreen, points away from the cane fields, diagonally across the strip and into the parchness of the bush. Game will be watching me now from inside the long, dry grass. They will be motionless like me, waiting for something to happen. I hitch my left leg over the gearstick and hoist it onto the seat. Only my heel makes contact, and my flesh feels the burning heat of the plastic. I bend my knee and find the whole thing more comfortable. I search the white-fleeced clouds for movement and listen into the wind for engine-sound. I yawn, and hold the flat of my hand in front of my mouth for no one else but myself. There should be more of life like this – a complete rest. It is such moments as these that one looks back on as happiness but rarely appreciates at the time. Are these moments the reason for our lives? The peace of solitude is a great comfort amid the turmoil of life.

I lean across and pull my old bush hat from under the dashboard. The brim pulls flat and shields my eyes from the piercing glare of the sun. To someone else my eyes look almost shut, yet I see to a great distance down the thousand feet of runway and out over the bush to the red hills of the escarpment. A dove pu-purrs from the bush on the other side of the strip. I listen. There are more further in. The whole valley is dotted with the purring doves sitting in their separate trees. The valley is content like me. There is no movement, neither in the sky, nor the bush, nor the cane fields. We watch the day. I hear the crackling dryness and feel the insects moving among the fallen leaves and dried sun-beaten grass. Nothing grows in there at this time of the year – no rain.

A kudu comes out of the bush and stands looking at me across the expanse of dry, flat earth. The great antlers balance her grace and her knot-ended tail sweeps up and down and to and fro. Her head goes up as she tries to get my scent. I look at my rifle but don't wish to disturb the peace. She turns and crashes back into the bush and the sound of her flight grows fainter and fainter.

An aero-engine filters into my straining ears. I turn my head and shoulders and search the sky. A silver streak comes towards me from the depth of blue sky. I look back at the wind sock – there is no wind to fill its sausage – it hangs. The single engine fights with the last mile of air. The engine pitch heightens. The plane drops fast and flattens out above the leafless trees and hurls itself at the runway. The slipstream catches up the dust and sprays it behind. The front wheels hit and the green and silver plane bump, bump, bumps onto earth and rushes past me. The engine howls in its agony. The tail drops and the plane slithers and slows with the brakes to a stop. The propeller screams but the plane doesn't move. Only the dust is airborne in a long line behind the plane's mechanical embrace with earth. The engine revs, the plane slows round to point at me and gets bigger. The thatch-topped hanger is behind me. I parked the Land Rover so I couldn't see its roof on the four heavy gum poles. I wave as the Cessna 172 goes past me. Max waves from the cockpit. There are three other people in the plane – one at least, by the length of hair, is a woman. I turn my head away to avoid the dust cloud but the dry musty smell goes up my nose and into my lungs. I stretch my left hand forward past the black steering wheel to the ignition key and press the starter motor. I drive forward and circle round and follow the aircraft, parallel to its hanging dust trail. The peace of the bush is completely destroyed. The plane slews again and noses under the shade of the rough thatch.

Some of them will have to sit in the back of the Land Rover on the metal ridges either side of the truck. There is room for two passengers in the front. The engine cuts and the propeller runs its speed down to become visible. I stop the truck and climb over the Land Rover's door. The dust and noise floats away to settle and disappear. A small door opens in the side of the Cessna and a foot comes out backwards and gropes for the rung it knows is there… And finds it. Max steadies himself and jumps the three feet. He holds his hands up to the open hatch. Doris Whitman leans out, face first, and falls into his arms. He puts her down with ease as I walk across in the sun.

"Hello, Doris. I didn't expect to see you so far from the big city. How was the flight, Max?"

Two others follow my one-night stand.

"This is Dudley Cooper and Sheila Hamilton, a friend of Doris's. You know Doris. Dudley's here to look at the sugar for his company in Canada. We hope to cut his costs by selling direct to his chain stores from the refinery. I think he'll get a better idea of why we are able to sell so cheaply when I show him how we grow the stuff."

"Goo'day. Hello, Sheila. Give me those bags. You came light."

"I didn't want to overload the plane with four passengers. Dudley's a big man."

"Will the girls get in the front with me? This is the bush, Mr. Cooper, so you'll have to try the back. It isn't very comfortable on the rough roads."

"Call me Dudley, Guido. So, that's what it looks like when it's growing. We've eighty-seven stores throughout Canada so we can do with a whole lot of sugar at the right price. I like roughing it for a change. The air smells real fresh up here and the sun's real hot. I'm glad you brought me up, Max. I'm going to enjoy these few days. What do you say, Sheila?"

She smiles at him.

"I don't know exactly where we're going to put you as we have four guests already, but if you don't mind doubling up in the bedrooms we'll be all right. I should have shot a kudu I saw just now to put some meat in the fridge. Maybe you'd like to come out with us this evening, Dudley, while we hunt some game? Max usually comes out if he has time. The girls won't mind you leaving them for a couple of hours. You'll have to shoot on my licence and say you're carrying my extra gun. If you shoot legally it costs too much. We first walk back to the Land Rover empty-handed of guns and game, look around for the game warden skulking in the bush and then drive to the kill. If they catch you on the open road it's just bad luck. I've been having a friendly war with the Game Department for ten years. It adds to the interest. We'll drive straight to my house for breakfast. I'm sure you're all hungry."

# 16

*E*ven deep in the bush, without any sign of civilisation – even the tracks made by elephant – Max can't forget business. His mind swims in calculations and pending decisions. There is no peace for him – but maybe he doesn't want any. He uses anyone's brain as a springboard. He sucks out their intelligence in a rush of urgency and high tension and makes it appear as though helping him is an honour and achievement. His is the road to modern success – for this there is no need to be brilliant. It requires only the ability to marshal the facts from other people.

The Canadian is over to my left and moving forward with the .375 slung forward and pointing up the glade of tall-trunked trees over the elephant grass. The thorn bushes clutch at his legs when he doesn't watch where he is walking.

I can see for half a mile either side where the slopes rise through the trees. In front, the trees merge in the distance.

Dudley Cooper searches the far trees and grass and thorn bush for the game he doesn't believe is here. He has a smooth, round face – the fat probably hid his chin when he was a child. His hair has receded on both sides of his pate and left a tuft of insecurity dead centre. He is heavy and stumbles through the bush, whereas Max, right beside me and in the full flight of his monologue on the prospects of turning part of Gokwe into a citrus estate, walks smoothly around the obstacles without apparently noticing them. By the right of good hunting he should be out on my flank but Max finds it necessary to do more than one thing at a time.

"Guido, can't you say a little more than just yes or no and hum and ha? You must have some constructive ideas to add to what I'm saying."

"No, I think the idea is sound provided the price of citrus doesn't fall in the way that sugar has done in recent months."

"But this is the beauty of my plan. If the price of one goes down, the other may go up. We'll be concerned with two crops so the risk is spread. It's essential to go forward in a successful business. I investigated cotton and Burley tobacco but I couldn't find enough profit in them."

"I'm sure your deductions are correct, but I find it difficult to bring my whole mind to bear when I'm searching the bloody bush for game. They stand still and blend with the bush – you can walk past a herd of kudu."

"It doesn't really matter if we don't see anything. The walk will have done us good."

"When I come out for game, Max, that's all I'm doing. Like when I run the sugar estate I'm not dreaming about my next kudu. I didn't come for a walk, I came to shoot some meat."

"Your mind isn't flexible enough."

"That's most likely true but it's how I'm made. I suppose I could force it to think of your citrus and keep it searching the bush for game but if I did that I wouldn't get any pleasure out of either."

"How has Maralene been behaving herself?"

"Very well. She's a nice girl."

"She takes after her mother. I grew bored with her mother's solidness. You can't sit through life and do nothing about it. My second wife was the same after she'd spent as much money as she could and grown bored with the novelty. I suppose you haven't told the estate about your father and sister? Gwen is attractive. A mature girl for her age. I rather think she knows how life goes. Maralene tells me that at first there was something between you and Berna. Did you try and give it to her and get told your fortune? Shoot the bloody thing, Dudley! And again. Good shot. I like those small bush buck. They make good *biltong*. Kango! There's a job for you. Gut it and sling it over your shoulder. A bit more walking and we'll show you something bigger, Dudley. Can't have you going back to Toronto saying there isn't any big game in these parts. Now, where were we, Guido? Bloody silly killing one of those with a .375 but that's how it goes. I'll bet his shoulder hurts. Berna's a nice girl. Her father is class conscious and wouldn't like his daughter to marry a continental, but I'm sure that once he's heard of the Harrogate millions he'll be most amenable. They've plenty of money themselves. Yes, she's got almost everything that girl. I like your father. I told him I knew you were his son. Hope you didn't mind."

"I told him you knew the story."

"Anyway, he showed the correct amount of surprise. I'd like to see you married, Guido. It'd settle you down and stop you being so damned remote – bring your feet down to earth – give you some permanent responsibilities. I like to see every grown man with a wife and children. You'd produce some good-looking children, you and Berna, and that's always an asset. I wouldn't have brought Doris Whitman if I'd known what was going on. I'll tell Doris about Dudley's money and that he isn't married. The last bit should spark her interest. She wants to marry money. He is married, of course, but she'll find that out too late. Pity I wasn't born a woman – it seems an easy way to get rich. By the way, I told Jim he mustn't play around with other women on the estate. I don't like to see my senior employees doing things like that. It sets a bad example and enables the others to laugh at them. I think he saw the point. He'd find it difficult to get another job that's so well paid. Anyway, she's your sister so I was doing you a favour as well. Maralene told me about them. She also thought the game ranger was getting friendly with Stella but I really don't care. Jim might have got jealous and done something. Some things are better not said. It would help us if Doris let Dudley play around with her. Don't you think it's time we walked back to the Land Rover? You and Kango can take Dudley out another time. I'm glad we've had time for a chat. Dudley! We're going back. The light'll go soon. We don't have any twilight in this country. Yes, Doris can soften him up and in the end it'll be us who make the money. By the way, I told Sheila that Gordon Harrogate was a millionaire widower – it made her eyes roll. It should give your father some laughs."

"I don't think he's made that way."

"Of course he is. It'll wake up his vitals. If we need more capital for the citrus he can be very helpful. Ah, Dudley, that was some good shooting. You must have had experience in the war or something. Tell me, would your company be interested in concentrated orange juice? We could put your brand label on right here at the factory. It would indicate to people that you owned a citrus estate as well as a sugar estate. It's the kind of advertising that makes you look bigger than you are."

"If the price is right, we can look into it. We might also be interested in canned fruit – grapefruit, naartjies, things like that – provided, as I said, the price is right. Let me put it this way – I'm interested in anything that undercuts our competitors and leaves us the same ratio of profit as before. Do you come into the business side of all this, Guido?"

"I only make sure we produce the quality as cheaply as possible."

They smile in their superiority and enable me to move away and walk the track four paces behind Kango. The buck's tongue hangs from its lolling head down his back. It makes me remorseful and yet if I order a steak in a restaurant I don't think of the slaughterhouse and the frightened eyes of death-sentenced cows and heifers – I don't think of the sheep lying twisted with their throats cut. But I do see this buck, vulnerable, dead and lolling, having changed its name to venison.

The bush is alive as the sun goes down – the zing of crickets mingles with birdsong. In the distance, baboons make obscene noises as they move about deep in the glades. The grass has turned to corn-yellow, the colour of Berna's hair. The air is cooling. The coming night separates us. The fear of darkness creeps into our minds. Civilisation is exchanged for a need to survive. Max stops talking and accepts the power of trees and shadow, the power of coming night, that makes us look for a tree to roost in or a hole to crawl into or a fire to bring us light and security. This, all around me, is basic, unfuddled, uncluttered by the irrelevances of modernity. Here I am whole and complete. I fear what my instinct fears. My mind doesn't look for eternity.

It is too dark to see game. The bush accepts us as it will the elephant on their way down to drink at the river. It will preserve all secret places and everything will live in fear of the night that protects it. Dudley and Max hold their guns more fiercely. My rifle rests easily across the back of my shoulders, held at the muzzle by my left hand. My feet move lightly and the cool air goes down into my lungs. This night is freedom. The pace of our walking has quickened. The dead animal flops in sympathy with Kango's movement. The trees I blazed pass one by one. It's too dark to track our spoor.

THE LAND ROVER is just ahead. Max and Dudley are pleased. It has always been like this – I answer to the hereditary of my civilisation.

I check the safety catch and press my .375 into its pads and get into the driver's seat. Kango gets into the back and the others climb in beside me. My left hand comes up to the key. I wait a moment, listening to the wilds. I viciously stab the starter and shatter the bush with man-made noise. The headlights flick on easily and stab violently into the new night and destroy some of it. I rev, gear and roll us forward. We are civilised gentlemen.

## 17

"Dad, would you like some more brandy?"

"Thanks, son. It's nice being on our own. That fellow Max can't sit still for five minutes. Exhausts me. Hope I wasn't like that at his age. No sooner had he propelled us through the dinner party than he was off to the club. I don't think he liked you not falling in with his plans but you were right to stick out if you didn't want to go. Pleading age for me is always a winner. A lack of youth has its advantages. The mosquitoes don't bite me since I rubbed on that damn lotion. Science has its advantages too. No, you've got to be firm with the Maxes of this world or they'll ruin your life. I've been thinking during these last couple of weeks that maybe I should make Harrogate Falls a public company. I can offer fifty-one per cent of my shares through the stock exchange and stay on as chairman without the same responsibilities. Then I can relax in the way I've been able to here. It'll give others an interest in the company. They'll want some new blood on the board of directors who'll stop the company sliding as I get older. Now you won't come back there's little point in trying to keep everything. If I sold outright or let myself be merged with someone else, I'd lose my position – but not this way. How does it sound?"

"Sensible. There's a point where all the struggle isn't worth it – and we don't get younger – me as well as you. You'll have time to come out here when the weather gets cold in England. You'll always be welcome."

"I've enjoyed myself, really enjoyed myself here and it isn't something one often does in life. I've had snatches of peace before, but not often for so long. I think this is what I should have looked for in my life but it's not an easy thing to concentrate on in the turmoil of business and industry. This brandy's good. It's nice to drink it without having to warm it. Have one of my cigars. I know you don't smoke very much but they complete the relaxation.

"I don't think you and Max will last in business if you have to work close to each other. He wants to dominate everything and he can't do this with you. He's good – I can see it – the kind of energy one needs at the top of big business. But he mustn't have someone of equal calibre below him or there's sure to be friction. I've been watching these things for years. The first need in business is staff harmony – and to achieve this you must employ the right combination of personalities and brains. A good brain can't tolerate incompetence above or below and a leader can't be led or thwarted by juniors. This selection is the art of chairmanship. For you to be able to work successfully with Max, he must hold something over you and give you an income you can't afford to lose. But what money do you need as a bachelor? As it is, his need to make money is irrelevant to you – your purpose in life is different. People who matter to him he thinks he can change to his purpose. He thinks this with you. He thinks he can force you to conform, but I know he can't as I tried myself with a far richer prize as my catalyst. Money will never be your god as you have never foreseen insufficiency.

"At your age, and much younger, I thought money would buy what I wanted and to some extent it did – but now that I've had it for so long the fear of losing it has gone and the only need left is power. But what is power without a purpose? What's the use of power in itself? The trouble is that one's real purpose changes in life but it's not always possible to reorientate the same life to comply with the new need and so the old purpose is pursued towards the inevitable destruction – that inevitability being the ultimate death. The needs of life change in us constantly but the mainstream of our lives goes on from the impetus given to it at the start of our careers. This is the product of specialisation. In some cases the career can be divorced from the private life but in commerce and industry this is becoming less and less true and the pattern of life is even more difficult to change once it has been made and the material needs enjoyed. You, as very much the exception, have tried and so far largely succeeded in forcing your career to conform with your private life. I admire you for this, and wish, looking back, that I had had been able to do the same – but it wasn't possible in England. Here there is so much space. At home there was no room to move from the mainstream.

"Yes, a few weeks out here would be something to look forward to. Are you going to get married again one of these days?"

"Yes... Yes, I'm sure I will eventually. Life wouldn't be complete without a wife and children. But one need can hinder another. With an expensive wife and a brood of kids I might become beholden to Max and then my freedom would be lost – and it's this that I value more than anything. With freedom of mind and movement and with just sufficient material needs any problem can be discarded and any embarrassment ignored. Civilisation doesn't suffocate a free person, a person who is free of all other people and needs nothing from them materially or emotionally. There are few free people in the world. For myself, I have never met one. And this reliance is necessary in a family. It was to feed this need that civilisation was built. And as it built itself so it destroyed our instincts and made us force ourselves to be different to what we are. Civilisation destroyed freedom by the very nature of itself. In great art this fog created by our society is removed and the real purpose of life revealed. But even then the reason for existence is only felt, it isn't understood. Maybe without civilisation this question of eternity would never have come up and happiness would have been maintained within the walls of instinct. Life would only have been natural. Its purpose would have been revealed as it was needed and the mind of man would only have concerned itself with reality. Life would have been lived for itself and not as it is now, for what it might be in the future if something changes, out of our control, but changes so the utopia envisaged by our modern minds becomes a miraculous reality. Modern life has created a sea of red herrings. To remain out of the sea I must remain free and if I let one of my instincts have its reign I will find myself with Berna but I will destroy the other need without which I won't have a life but only its mirage. So I go on as I am – losing, but having some answer to the roots of my own mind."

"Why don't you get away from this and set yourself up on your own?"

"I've thought of that. During the last boom a man called Alex Storp got irrigation rights about forty miles downstream. The country was importing bananas from Mozambique and the government thought five hundred acres growing on the banks of the Zambezi would reduce their foreign exchange. He only planted one hundred acres before he went bust. His lorry fell to pieces over the eighty miles of dirt to the main road and during the rains his bananas rotted on the trees as the road was impassable. His place has been on the market for years – I could get the lot for fifteen hundred pounds. The banana groves would be overgrown but a little extra capital would get his irrigation equipment working well enough to grow two hundred acres of cotton. I wouldn't make a fortune, but the price of cotton is stable and I wouldn't need to bow and scrape to anyone to sell it. And if the price of cotton falls below an economical level I could grow maize or something else. There's a reserve close by who'd supply the cotton pickers. The crop has to be sprayed eleven times during the season – I thought of buying an old aircraft. They won't bother about a certificate of airworthiness, if I only flew over my own crops. I could maintain it myself and bring out a mechanic once a year to give it the major overhaul. I'd be self-contained. It's an idea. If I fall out with Max then I've something to fall back on. I think this is what I've hankered towards during the years in the valley – to be alone and by myself. Becoming managing director here has given me some control over my freedom but there's still Max, and Max and I, as you say, are not compatible in the present arrangement. Anyway, I have the money now, thanks to this job."

"Is Max still married?"

"No, not anymore. Maralene was born to his first wife. The second marriage was childless."

"He's got his eye on Gwen. She's old enough to do what she likes but I think his experience is too much for her. She finds him different to the undergraduates, which he is."

"I'll mind him to keep his filthy habits away from her. He's lecherous and uses women to further his ends. He set Doris Whitman on me when I started this job to see if I'd join the set, to see if I needed money for that. I enjoyed the evening but for healthy reasons only. He's using her now to get a contract from the Canadian. He's dangled your money at Sheila in the hope of finding you vulnerable – he thinks he may need more loan capital for his new project. He doesn't miss a bloody trick. It would please his ego to seduce Gwen. He'd think he'd finally got at me. And in a way he would have done. He's the typical, modern success story."

## 18

"Is your seatbelt fastened properly, Maralene? Needn't ask you, Guido. No, Berna, let me put it down a little. It's more effective further down and I shouldn't like anything to happen to you. There, that's much firmer. You've got a nice pair of hips. Checks completed and revs up so here we go. It's a bit cold but you'll see this early morning flying is worth it when we get up in the sky. We should see some game. Your sister and I, Guido, saw plenty of buffalo yesterday."

We move forward and turn to face down the still and silent runway. My father was right. Max'll go to any lengths. He'll even go for Berna, who's less than half his age, to make me interested in her. And so he does. She likes older men. She told me that herself. What does it matter anyway? I'll buy that rundown banana plantation and go and find myself some peace. Too many people upset my equilibrium and make me want things I didn't want before.

We gather speed and the runaway rips along underneath us. The small plane fights the rough surface and Maralene falls against me despite her harness – I put my arm around her shoulder and we take off together. Like a tripped switch, the jolts go out and we fly.

We go higher and higher and looking down, our speed seems less and less. She doesn't move so I keep my arm where it is to annoy her father. We fly on in the morning. The sun, over to my left, is watching the valley and river from just above the escarpment range. The trees are small down there and the faint, irregular lines of the elephant tracks are difficult to trace. The black line of the main road slashes the bush in half. The early sun glints from the water and shines up the suspension bridge. With my free hand I undo my safety belt and relax. She fumbles with hers so I loosen it and brush her navel just above the top of her hipsters. I look at her sideways. She's looking at me. She smiles and I give her one back. I think she pushed her stomach forward on purpose. I wonder if Berna will go to Max so easily? I didn't sleep properly last night.

We drone on over the bush, along the course of the river. It's wild down below – nothing is cultivated. The bush is owned by the game and the tsetse fly and they keep it that way. I watch for the black, darker patches of game among the trees on either side of the river. Over there is Zambia. It doesn't look any different. Nothing is down below now. Up here it's me and Max and two young girls but down there they don't care. Max pushes the plane lower and the trees separate themselves and rush along underneath us. I search hard for game as if I hadn't seen any before – I don't want to think. Two elephants look straight up at me and I point and everyone leans forward to look and Max dips our left wing at the game and Maralene spreads herself across my lap for a better view and runs her firm, young, left breast down my right arm and this time I'm sure it's on purpose. There must be something in this valley that makes us like this. The bull elephant flaps his ears as we soar past him and I'll bet he never asks the question of how we got here.

There is sun and sky out through the Perspex but nothing else, not even a heat haze. We cast no shadow on the river nor bush – the sun isn't high enough.

I heard Gwen come in last night and turned on my bedside lamp after she'd gone upstairs. It was two o'clock and the club closes by midnight as the barmen have 'set' hours if there isn't an organised party. They have their own lives to lead like anyone else. Everyone feels better for the rule the next morning. She and Max came back together and alone. Maybe they like each other so who am I to judge Max by what I do in such circumstances myself? Just because I have always taken out women and tried to bed them doesn't mean that Max is the same – but I doubt if he isn't.

"There they are, Max, well in under the trees over there."

I point across Maralene and she pushes up to rest her sweatered front on my arm so she can see better. I pull back my arm, rubbing it firmly against her. The plane banks and circles towards the motionless herd of buffalo in among the trees. They look so tame and powerless from up here – like cows. Yet I know they're not. The bush doesn't have any feeling or reality from up here and the buffalo are toys.

The back of Berna's neck is soft and Maralene's shoulder is still touching me. Gwen may have got it last night or he may have given it to her before. I may not be able to get away from Max. He may have influence with the Water Board and I'll get my plantation but no irrigation rights. I must be getting old and, then again, I didn't sleep very well last night. With Berna by myself down there it would be different but these things don't happen like that. Better to let it all go on as it is and play the cards as they come. Life's short and I've lost half of it now and the other half is none too sure to stay waiting for me. Can I, as one person, change even my own life?

Max banks hard and we fly out into Rhodesia at right angles to the Zambezi. We fly over the bush were no one goes except the game rangers and poachers. It's a big valley. The sun is now flitting a slanted shadow of us over the jungle. My head aches with too many of my own problems.

The seats are very small and close together. The throttle, like a car's handbrake lever, thrusts between Berna and Max, challenging them with its phallic symbolism. He flies the plane easily. The propeller in front of the screaming engine obscures nothing in its speed. I sit back and try and let the tension drain out of me. I try to draw myself down to be inside this plane and part of it and the company. I try to think of Berna as something to be overpowered physically and thrust into, instead of the image I have made.

"Shall we return for some breakfast? We're just as likely to see game on the way back. I don't like flying too far into nowhere without any water on board."

We go up a little and bank round and the sun glints in through the Perspex and sears my eyes and we swing further and away from it and hope we are pointing back to the river. This is Max's problem for a change. Let him have it. The bush is all the same below, no landmarks, nothing. We begin to climb.

"Better find out where we are. If we get up a bit we'll see the river and the estate. Better to be sure now than sorry later. How are you feeling, girls? Nothing like a morning flip now is there?"

Our field of vision increases and I wait for the landmarks to come out of the new heat haze. He never takes chances, which is how it should be. I would have flown on just above the trees with the added excitement of possibly going the wrong way tormenting me silently until we either ran out of fuel or crossed the river.

The escarpment range shows first and now the river. The flatness of cultivation is over there. And we are going the wrong way. The plane banks and sets course for the river.

# 19

"Maralene, I think it's better if you and Berna come and stay in the house here. There isn't any point in you continuing to bother the Marshams. I'll have a couple of rooms cleaned out. Just as well you didn't move into my house, Guido, as I suggested. Gives me somewhere big to put up my guests. Do you mind moving your room, Sheila, so the girls can be next to each other?"

"We've been sharing a room at the Marshams, so don't move around just for us. But it would be nice staying here with the swimming pool."

"It's not civilised to share a bedroom, Berna, and there's more than enough room now we're using this house. Sheila can sleep in the one next to Dudley and I'm sure neither of them will mind about that. Now, who wants more breakfast? Cheer up, Guido, it probably won't happen."

But on the other hand it probably will. He must have had Gwen, too, to want to move Berna in here. I think he considers every attractive woman as an insult to his age. I wonder what his blood pressure is like. Probably stronger than mine! People like that don't have problems. I would have been better to stay as the unknown Guido Martelli, keeping the electricity running and finding my women where I went. I have only gained a new set of problems and in no way achieved any permanency in the valley. If I answer truthfully, I am less in control of my life now. Then my unsolved problems could be looked at and turned over for better inspection but now my mind cavorts in and out of itself. Soon I'll join the sea with all the other red herrings and nothing but my own petty needs will matter anymore. The need for pure freedom is not petty. The desire to look forward and through to the infinity of existence is not either. The desire to reach down and understand the reason for existence is basic and in the natural saps and roots and instincts of us all. But it may not come up because they say so and the Maxes of this world hold the power in trust for the likes of them. It is the system. I don't feel sorry for myself anymore – I am part of the system and it has made life the same for all of us and allowed us the freedom of sex to express ourselves and sully our souls in its excess – because without procreation we die out. This one they couldn't change.

I eat the bacon and kidneys and slurp at the fresh coffee but it doesn't taste the way it used to on my roof veranda by myself with the whole world of cane and valley drawn out in front of me to the sun. My soul is sick – here is the crux and there is no remedy in science or quacks for this. It is an ailment in the essence of my being and it has just shown me that it is stronger than me. I must live with it. I must play with it and let it run its course of pranks and hopes. I must become normal in the extent of joining everyone else's insanity and purpose. I must fit into this society and enjoy my breakfast.

How much the Africans have got to fear if they only knew it. Better they don't. Better to hope the emergence from instinct is good. Many will go through the new life in great expectation and many of the sick souls won't be diagnosed even by themselves. The heart of existence will be dead in them as it is in so many of us, is almost dead in me. How much courage do I need to get up and go out of here and make my final peace with the big river? Too much, as they have shown me too much and clouded the course of my purpose. Eleven years in the wilderness and nothing to show for it but a bad appetite and a sick soul that no one can see. My peace would be by the river but this can never be allowed by them or else society would be proved wrong. The musicians can express the sickness of a man's soul and show its darkness to those who understand because those who don't know won't know what to interpret. They won't be able to see 'the revolt' and cut out the canker of its freedom and instinct as they cut out communism or capitalism, whichever their inclination. We are brainwashed to a freedom that is bound by the shackles of society. The prone red herring of democracy is given to us to play with at election times and as a sop to nature there are the Elios and Stella Marshams and the Doris Whitmans and whoever comes next on the list. The mind can be sick provided the body is firm. The strange accidents of life can be regimented and fitted into the strange hysterics away from the river. There is no purpose to life because man doesn't want one. We must go on fornicating and procreating to keep the whole thing going so we can pass the riddle on. No, not quite a riddle – a riddle has an answer.

"I'll have some more of your coffee, Max. The second cup always tastes best to me. You must give me some flying lessons before you go back to Salisbury. I'll have to go into the office after this but I can find time this afternoon to take out whoever wants to go on the river. I can usually bring the estate up to date with three hours' work. I rarely sit down in my office – moving around keeps my brain working faster. Anyone who has a problem writes it down and I either give the answer into the Dictaphone or use the telephone. It's a case of always being up to date so as not to be busy and have time to spare when it is needed. Organisation is essential in modern business. I'll have a driver sent over to the Marshams to collect your clothes. Now, if you'll all excuse me, I must get on with some work. If you require any more details of shipping costs come to my office when you're ready, Dudley. This month's cost sheets will be ready by eleven. Max, I'll have a copy sent up to you here."

This is how I must be. I mustn't let my better emotions suffocate my mind. I push back the chair and give the room a broad smile for everyone and press my stiff napkin onto my bread-crumbed side plate. It behaves as it should and doesn't spring onto the floor. I walk down the long room and out of the double glass doors onto the veranda. The sun sears into my eyes and I slit them almost shut, the half-grin at the morning and the cane-nodding sprays. I feel the back of my head and twist my index finger into my right ear for no reason at all. All this is the same. The cane hasn't changed. Nothing has changed from the outside.

"These production figures are good, Guido. You're crushing almost to the maximum. I once had figures like these. I don't often find people doing so well in my absence. You've made a success of this job. If the price of sugar increases we'll begin to make the right kind of profit. Your father tells me he is going back to England tomorrow. He's booked on a plane. I think it has something to do with my late interest in Gwen but I can't be sure of these things. Women always want too much and are never grateful for what they get. I'll have to take a closer look at Berna since you're not interested. Mustn't let the old sap go down. She's very attractive. In the prime of her looks. Oh, and I know what you're thinking – I know she's my daughter's age but one can't look a gift horse so sexually appetising as that in the mouth."

"You know something, Maximillian Rosher, you're about the lowest bastard I've come in contact with."

"Hey, don't you talk to me like that, Sonny Jim."

"I'll talk to you as I like, Sonny Jim, and I'll even hold you against the bloody wall if you try and get away from what I've got to say to you. Oh, and don't look so cocksure about your physical prowess – at this point in our ages you and I are not matched. You're getting old, Max, and too flabby for a roughhouse. I'd enjoy throwing you at the wall and I'd enjoy seeing the three false teeth you so cleverly conceal coming out and showing the gaps in your manly appeal. So you think you can go to any lengths to force people to your will. You think by seducing my sister and making a fool of my father you can make me crawl to you. And if that isn't enough, you go for the one woman you think I'm interested in, in the hope I'll ask you, the 'big boss', if you'll lay off because I want her and I'm prepared to prove it by getting married and conventionally settling down. You want her big papa brought into it so Guido Martelli will change to Mark Harrogate in public so after that he'll be too scared to tell you to get stuffed for fear of losing his big job that keeps him up there with papa and able to pamper papa's little daughter. You'd even eat shit if it made you enough money! Now get out of my office while I collect what belongs to me. I was nearly over the line of no return but not quite. You oozed in here just in time to save me. You can stuff my job right up your arse and I hope it makes you constipated."

"So you think you've become the big boy. Well, well. It comes to most of them in the end but in the end they find out they're mistaken. You think there are still some things about you I don't know but I make it my business to know everything. I have a file for you all which even tells me what key you fart in. You think your bare-bottom slapping with Mrs. Stella Marsham is a secret of yours and hers only – oh, and there's a jealous man is Jim. All the guns under the table won't help you in the dark of the night, if he decides to carve up your profile with a razor – just think of it slicing your flesh. Nice shooting, Mr. Martelli, but I could have told our burnt-out friend there was a gun under that table and that it had lived there for three years against Jim and his predecessors. Nothing is news to me on the sugar estate, even your discreet little enquiries about the price of Alex Storp's overgrown banana trees – which, incidentally, I bought for one thousand pounds six months ago. So, if you want to stay in the valley you're stuck with me and from now on I'll see you work a little harder. I don't like my employees taking the afternoons off without my permission. Good morning, Mr. Martelli, and don't think too hard about Berna. They say virgins don't please very much so you can have her after me. I rather like them as young as that. They tickle my ego and prove that my age is still young."

I lunge at him. He runs for the door. I chase him down the passage and out of the building. I crunch the gravel as he grabs and opens and slams his car door. He waves brightly for the benefit of witnesses as his tyres spin and he shoots forward and out of my reach.

I walk back past the African at the telephone exchange and I smile at him for the sake of appearances. There's more to going now than price and yet nowhere to go. He will have Berna if I leave and discard her like the rest and leave her like the rest – and the rest will suck her into their hopeless little lives and stain her all over with the tarnish of permanent unhappiness – like Elio. I walk through the open door of my office and tread the thick pile of the red carpet. I sink into my chair and try to control my breathing. Jealousy is ridiculous – but how real. There isn't a way to get at Max Rosher. He has the system on his side.

I should go now. If I don't I will never again be able to think in terms of truth. I will always be acting to keep my place in the system and changing my thinking to make it look right to myself. But if I run now, where is there to go? The world is full of people. There's no freedom. It has seeped into the African air, where I thought it wouldn't.

There is a limit to the world of running away. Mistakenly, because I believe in perfection, I have shown I can make them money. So I must go on making this money until I am destroyed and then it won't matter. I will have no reason for the revulsion I have for him now. I will be accepted and have the right to seduce young girls. I shall be able to drive off the bush track to the club and draw up with the right type of smile and be modern and enjoy myself. There's nothing to fight. We can't all run away to the Big River as there isn't enough room.

The polished table and clean, green blotting pad look up at me impersonally and wait for me to continue. Let's all go on without a purpose. My father will die without a valid reason for his life and I will follow him. What the hell else is there for me to do? It has always been this slow, seething desire to grab and slap down, to slither over and suffocate, to drown someone quietly to get more and more, to grab and have more for self, to slide up the greasy ladder with back-stabbing knives in both hands and the flag of reason, of freedom, of liberty, of Almighty Right fluttering stiffly and imperiously from the top. I should laugh, of course, but there isn't any laughter inside of me. I thought for twenty years there was more to life than what I see around me but there isn't.

Max needs me here. I can have this job so long as I keep up the work. Provided the profit is made, the words don't matter. I must accept Berna for what she is and prevent myself hoping for something deep. I won't have to see much of Max if I stay. He's often away. This is the first time he's come up since I took over and the board meetings in Salisbury are every two months and he isn't always there. I'll still be able to walk the bush. I should have realised before I reached thirty-five years of age that life won't change. I must grab the slippery pole, and when people aren't looking run off for a while.

## 20

"Throw some more wood on the fire, darling. Lots of crackling and flames reassures me against the barks and grunts. The whole bush sounds alive around us."

"Only hippo charge fires and they can't run up that hill so we're safe here on top of the riverbank. And no one would ever look for us this far downriver at night. I prefer it. There's the problem of getting back unnoticed but for the moment I can enjoy your company without keeping my ears permanently pricked. I can relax. Shall I cook you another piece of steak?"

"Yes, I'm hungry. It tastes good cooked over the wood fire."

"I'm glad we brought food. It makes the night more permanent."

I place the thin steak on the red-hot grill. It splutters viciously and starts to cook in its own fat.

"Do you think he'll tell Jim?"

"No. It won't gain him anything at the moment. He'll cash in when it suits him."

"When are his daughter and the other girl following him to Salisbury?"

"When they want to or when he thinks about it. He didn't have room for more than the Canadian and his Dolce Vita troupe in the plane. Poor Doris, she's really caught up in the rat race and she'll always get the runt end of the party. She hasn't enough brains to see how they use her or how to turn it to her own advantage. I think Sheila does it for cash or kind now – which is much more sensible for her. She wept on Dudley's shoulder about her debts at Barbour's department store. By the time he pays them off she'll have bought enough clothes to make him wonder whether the slap and tickle was worth it. He's plenty of money so why shouldn't he pay for her? She's nothing else to offer the world."

"Have I?"

"You don't offer it to the world for the moment. Or if you do I haven't found out. I must ask Max. He'll have it all down in his dossier."

"I don't really understand myself, but I haven't been after anyone else since I got here. I made a pass at Ted that night because I got mad at you ogling that Berna girl. You must satisfy my deeper moods. Turn that piece of steak over and give me a sip of your beer. I like Jim's police reserve duties. It gets rid of him for days on end and when he comes back I find he's not so bad after all. By then I've had lots of you and I'm all nice inside and satisfied and I'm happy with everyone. Was Gwen's affair with Max the reason your father left with her so quickly?"

"Partly. There was his company to think about as well. I suppose the whole estate knows he's my father."

"Max put it out on the grapevine. Said you'd done it so it didn't look to the world as though you'd got somewhere through influence."

"I suppose Max thought it would increase the image of me as the 'big boss' of Gokwe. He never misses a chance. There was more to my reasoning than that, Stella, but I don't want to spoil the night by going into detail. Is that done enough? The salt's behind you on the rug. I like kudu steak a bit red. Only buffalo should be done well."

As she eats, the flickering firelight plays in the curves and hollows of her face. Another log crashes into the heat of the embers and flares its lighted tongue into the bush behind us, away from the river. The yellow tongues shrink towards us as the flame dies. The reflection flickers in her eyes. I tear a piece off my steak and eat. Some of the grease dribbles onto my chin. I push it into my mouth with the back of my finger and grab hold of the grease-smeared beer bottle and drink. The night and crackling fire and silent, moving river mass is all there is. There aren't any mosquitoes at this time of the year and there isn't any moon. The river is visible because of its smoothness and the faint ripple on its waters from the stars. The firelight doesn't reach down to the water nor reflect in the red eyes of crocodiles. What a peace this all is. I drink again and tear off more meat with my teeth and chew. I think I would have taken to my heels without her. She is someone who accepts me without question and wants nothing in return. She gives me the comfort I need. We are happy as we are and look neither back nor forward. I have decided enough things for the moment so Berna must wait. I will rekindle the emotion I had for her when I am ready.

I went back to my own house for lunch this morning and was sorry to see the bags and cases lined up to go. I told Father so, and for a moment I felt I was his son. I enjoyed his stay. He says he will come back regularly. I lost this relationship by going away in the first place but there is always something to lose – and then he wasn't what he is now. He was more like Max in those days in England.

Gwen didn't talk so tritely about Oxford and politics at lunch, but this isn't surprising after getting so close to Max. I don't think she liked him but she couldn't get away from the physical draw of him wanting her. She was frightened and satisfied by the experience. She will now understand a little more of the truth of modern life if this is anything. Father will get over the embarrassment when he's back on his own familiar ground at home. Africa and this river will seem far away, as it will to Dudley Cooper and Sheila. Only I stay here because it is where I live and I know nothing better. It is only at times like these that I find comfort for my bones and mind. I hope by staying in the valley I will find more. I can hope and in hoping, there is some kind of future. I have been here ten years and each year has crept up on me by going from one into another.

While we were sitting with coffee on the roof veranda, with the garden-party shade holding the fierce sun away from us, I heard the aircraft and, a little later, saw it take off. Its silver reflection turned and sped off towards Salisbury. The only feeling I had was of relief because I didn't have to make a decision; and then a little while after, just as we were about to put the cases in the car for Gwen and Father, a messenger arrived with a note. If I had been thinking clearly I would have expected exactly what he wrote as emotion never controls of his actions unless there is profit to be made by prolonging it. Having a managing director walk out at short notice would have reflected adversely on Max and if he tried to say I was fired there are law courts and the truth even though my dismissal might have been substantiated. So, he treated it all as his joke and left the scene for Salisbury to let me simmer down. Well, this I have done to an extent. The perspective is more clear and he will know from now on to keep away from me as much as possible. Provided I maintain the production figures my purpose to him will be fulfilled.

I burnt the note with my lighter and a pure feeling of dislike. I was right. He'd eat any garbage if it made him enough money. And yet he'll be laughing in Salisbury now and mentally drinking to his little victory. 'My dear Guido,' he'd said, 'that was quite an exciting run down your corridor and, as I got myself and the car away without damage, my age and yours can't be so incompatible. I must get you a copy of the exercises I do each morning for eleven minutes. I hope you didn't believe what I said about Berna. She wouldn't have an old daddy like me no matter how hard I tried. And Gwen came to me, Guido, and I think we did each other some good. I only have your best interests at heart when I play my little pranks. I hope you won't feel so sore when we see each other at the next meeting in six weeks' time. I'll send for the girls when I've found a house in Salisbury. Normally I stay in Meikles but I'll rent something for a while. And I'll look after her, don't you fear, and keep her away from the wolves. If everything comes around all right, can I be the best man?' He didn't even bother to sign it.

It will be easier to accept. I dislike almost everything he stands for but does this matter? There is a need for acceptance in life. I am here still and have found the old peace after facing reality. I suppose they will suck me more and more into their system of greed but this must be part of the acceptance. Provided I remain aware of the danger and keep my soul to myself, I shall survive. If I don't, I shall die eventually like everyone else.

The zing of the crickets is powerful. My boat is sucking at the slight swell of water down by the river. The firelight goes up into the trees around us and tidemarks the branches and dry leaves with a dome of light. We are at the centre of this. She and I are free because we aren't legally tied to each other. We can walk away in different directions and think of nothing but the relationship we had together. We can only relive what happened, we don't have to worry about consequence and the need for legal disentanglement. We enjoy each other because we want to. We can walk away.

I drink hard out of the beer bottle and suck it dry. I could throw it away into the darkness but it would mark one more place with the flow of civilisation's garbage. There are so few places left free of empty bottles.

A pleasant tiredness creeps over my bones as I stare at the flickering flames. My knees are hunched up to my chin. My .375 rests within reach but I won't need it. The night noises are calling for soft sex and companionship for twos. She throws another branch on the fire and we watch the red-hot sparks spring up, flare up and float and die out. Flames lick along the new, dry wood. I get up and stretch. There's enough wood in the pile for the night's fire. I walk around to her side of the fire and she looks up at me softly. She hugs her knees. She leans back and smiles up at me. I can see the roundness and smoothness of her breasts half inside the bra and soft green silk of her shirt. Her legs and thighs are bare to her hips and the shorts are pulled up to their limit. I kiss her gently and feel the softness and gentleness of her lips. Her hair is longer now and falls back behind the nape of her neck. I stroke it and think she purrs.

"I'm just going to check the boat's tie-ropes and then it's time for sleep."

"Don't be long."

"Don't go off with anyone else while I'm away."

"I love you."

"Those words don't mean anything anymore. This feeling is too rare to be called by that. Open me another beer for when I come back."

I kiss her again and feel the shape of her mouth. I put my hand down and pick up the .22 revolver from the rug, and begin to walk down to the water. I am soon into the night. I look back over my shoulder. The firelight dances about her. The campfire crackles. She gets up and waves before searching in the wet sack for another cold beer.

The sand loosens as I reach the first dune. There is enough moon to show me the lurking crocs. I go silently. I walk down a small sand dune and up another. The gun is in my right hand as my head comes over the crest. To my left, where the hoofmarks were thickest this morning, a big, heavy-shouldered eland is drinking. Royal game. Beside him and a little nearer to me are a pair of reedbuck – the female's horns are small and dainty in contrast to the power of the bull's as he drinks at the flowing edge. An elephant stands just inside the bush on the Zambian side. It took me five years to differentiate between game and thicket at that range. The wind is blowing from them into my face. The elephant crashes out of the bush and walks confidently down to the water. A baby elephant breaks cover and follows its mother. The mother trumpets to clear the path but nothing moves. The eland and reedbuck look across the protecting water and the small female runs back into the bush and stands perfectly still. The graceful horns of the bull point down again and the small tongue and nose touch the cool water. The water thrashes swiftly and violently and the buck reels under a blow. I run down the dune and fire a quick, accurate shot at the scaly lump snapping at the stunned buck. The eland has gone. The river flows on peacefully to the crash of retreating elephant. I stop short of the buck as it picks itself up. Its feet flounder in the sand and water. The crocodile's tail is vicious. I fire at the water and the bullet spurts a tail into the stars' reflection. Crocs are mostly cowards so it wasn't really necessary. The big horns shake above the small, delicate head and the feet find enough firmness to let him move away from me, picking up speed until he runs into the bush and safety.

I walk down to the boat and check the tie-ropes to the rock outcrop. A fish rises and plops back before I have time to look. The excitement runs out of me. I thrust the gun into the top of my shorts and walk back across the sand to the dome of fire-lit peace.

"What was it?" floats down to me.

"A crocodile."

"I don't like them."

"Neither do I." The night is normal again. In a little while other animals will come down to the river to drink, fearful, but unaware of this. I climb up the bank and feel the pressure of the calves of my legs. The barrel of the revolver sticks into my thigh. I top the bank and walk in under the tall trees that flank the length of the river at flood-water mark.

"There's always a drama close to you, Guido."

She laughs and hands me the beer. I swallow the first three inches. I pull out the gun, put it down on the rug and sit down next to her. I lie back and look up at the stars through the lacework of leafless trees high above me. I spread my right arm on the rug behind her. She looks down at me and the firelight shows me her tensity. My arm comes up and grips her and pulls her hard on top of me so I can feel all of her. She has taken off her pants.

I WAKE with the first light and the vague memory of having kept the fire stocked during the night. I smooth the hair away from her ear and put my tongue inside. She wakes and tries to get closer to me. I pull the blanket over her properly and get up. The water is out in front of me. It seems much closer than last night and smells of fresh weeds. A fish eagle circles above it looking for edible debris. The escarpment hills are black – the light hasn't any colour. The fire is still hot. I throw on handfuls of dried twigs and white smoke curls into the still air. I blow and the flames burst out and consume the smoke and some of the twigs. I put on some larger pieces and then the grill. I gurgle water from the demijohn into the pan, put it on the grill and watch the flames lick over the metal and into the water. A film of ash collects on the surface of the water. I clean two cups with sand and water and sit watching the birth of the sun.

The sun rims its way up over the escarpment as the water bubbles behind me. A teaspoonful of coffee goes into each cup, then the boiling water, powdered milk and sugar.

"It's a good morning, Stella. You're missing the best of it. Here's some coffee to wake you up. I'll cook some breakfast when I've washed in the river. There isn't any bilharzia in this part of the Zambezi. To think how many mornings I've slept through the dawn and wasted it."

"You're right. It's beautiful... And new. Doesn't the river look friendly? I slept well and didn't dream a thing. The coffee's good. Just as well no one can see us – as I'm naked. I see you pulled on your shorts."

"I dislike running away from elephants without my pants on. I'll take the rod and catch a couple of bream for breakfast."

"I like them fresh. I'll follow you down myself – I need a bath."

"Don't giggle like that. The neighbours wouldn't like it."

The coffee is scalding hot and warms the inside of my stomach after the inertia of sleep. I survey the valley over Stella's head and drink my coffee. She sits hunched in the blanket, blowing away steam from her drink.

It's still cold. The sun is just above the escarpment and picking up glare. White light spreads into the lush yellow of early softness and spreads over the trees and hills that surround us. The call of birds heightens and the fish eagles shriek. The fear of darkness is over. The heat will build up in a little while.

I strap on a holster and slip in the black-metalled gun, and take the rod and bait out of the fork of a mfuti tree. The ants haven't got in at the worms, to my surprise. I finger them into life in their tobacco tin. I collect a box of .22 bullets, my hunting knife in its sheath, the gaff and a box of hooks and go down the animal walk, over the dunes and across to the moving water.

I walk out on the rock that holds the boat, and deposit my impedimenta. The sun is too low to let me see the fish swimming around in their feeding grounds. I kneel on one knee and select a worm and slither its fat body over the barbed hook. I stand up. The bait dangles – I flick the rod and cast into deep water. With my free hand I feel the gun and assure myself it moves freely. I slip it out once and thrust its barrel towards the fast flowing centre of the river. A fish nibbles my hook and I strike and the contrary movement tries to unbalance me. I laugh and the clean noise goes out and follows the flow of the river. The line jerks away as I put the revolver back and this time he's on for good. I give line and slowly build up the resistance and pull him in with the reel. He jerks away. I let him run. I bend down for the gaff and grip it with my left hand and put it between my knees. It's a bream. It breaks the surface and wallows with the hook in its mouth as I reel in strongly on the heavy, unfishermanlike line. It guggles its way along the surface towards me. I hold its head just out of the water, free my right hand, grip the rubber handle and hook the sharp end of the gaff into its gills and hoist it onto the rock beside me. It flaps desperately for a moment and then lies flat and fish-shop like. The water is full of bream – the sun has tipped enough light into the water. They are near the surface, circling and circling having never seen a hook, a line or man before. With one foot on the three-pound bream's head I search the water for the largest, see a big one, follow it, draw my right hand towards the .22 and as the fish touches the height of its circle I draw and fire from the hip, one after the other. Water-jets spurt in close inches around where I saw the fish and the visible surface is destroyed by the convulsions of bullets and fish. The six-shot magazine is empty. The fish rolls dead up to the surface and flows on down with the river. I whoop in delight, put the gun on the rock, grab the gaff and leap into the water to get on top of my fish. We both go down. I come up and look around for the crocs and the dead fish. I feel my knife in its sheath as I dog-paddle, keeping pace with the river. My fish bobs up beside me and I take careful aim with the gaff and chop at it with minute accuracy and delicacy. The fish sticks against the gaff's barb and we swim together. I kick my feet violently to discourage the crocodiles, swimming firmly against the river flow, and throw the gaff and fish onto the rock and pull myself dripping and happy out of the Zambezi.

"What the hell are you doing down there?"

"Catching fish."

"Sounds like a war."

"Come and have your bath. There won't be a croc around here for hours."

The hook comes out of my first fish easily. My knife slits its gut and its belly oozes out into the morning sun. Head, tail and innards of both fish follow each other into the water to delight the river scavengers. We have enough for our breakfast. I clean my hands of fish-gut and kneel down to the water with my shorts already wet and douse my head and trunk in the pure, clean-smelling swiftness of the river. It's cold and violent and draws the sinews of new life out of my good night's sleep and pleasure at being just where I am, with just who I want to be and not a damn thing else.

"Are you sure there aren't any crocodiles?"

"There are hundreds of them and each one of them has been waiting for Stella. Come here and let me grab you and feed you bit by bit to the crocodiles. I want to prove my cruel streak is as macabre as I think. Come and be vamped."

"I don't mind you being carnivorous but not in that way. I prefer the violence that shows your passion is roused."

"Well, it's roused now, so come here."

I grab at her and she shrieks in delight as I pick her up and swing her towards the water. I twirl round and gather momentum to launch her out into the river. She beats my chest and face with her fists so I fight my mouth down to hers and bite her lip and get the taste of blood. I slow as my momentum subsides with my concentration elsewhere and her legs slide down and we force our bodies at each other as hard as they'll go. She bites my lip and the bloods mingle in our mouths. I pick her up again and run at the water and jump in with the fish. We come up together shrieking and wallowing and me with my hand on my knife just in case and my eyes on the water around us.

"Have your wash while I keep the bath free of the other tenants."

"It's marvellous and fresh and, though I'm frightened to death, I'm loving every second of it. There goes my shirt... Now bra. Say, haven't I met you in the water before?"

I swim around with the knife in my right hand and she splashes and cleans away the aftermath of our night. I watch the water carefully, taking no chances. She swims to the rock and pulls herself up. The cloth of her shorts is no keeper of propriety. Her big, cold-firmed breasts stream water as she gets out. I follow her towards the rock.

"I'll race you to the fire."

I thrash at the last feet of water and tear myself out of it. She runs with her elbows high and her breasts swinging out almost to reach them. Her bottom-cheeks squeeze the water out of her shorts as she runs. I move quickly and smoothly over the sand and shorten the gap between us. She runs up the first dune and then disappears. I run faster and top the dune as she tops the second. She is shouting in fearful expectancy as she runs at the bank below the camp and stumbles up it.

"I'm catching you. I'm just behind you."

I grab her at the top of the bank and pin her arms behind her back with one hand and use the other to feel her nipples and then all over her body before picking her up and carrying her onto the rug.

THE RAYS of the sun cut across her stomach and throw her belly button into relief. Where do I get the energy from? There must be a little box of it inside me all ready for explosion. The sun is warm. I kiss her and get up and put some more wood on the embers for breakfast cooking and walk down to the river wearing my on-off pair of shorts. Surprisingly, the flies haven't found the fish. I wash them again and gather up the rest of my stuff. Soon it will be uncomfortable in the direct line of the sun without a hat. The sand is hot under my bare feet as I walk back with the fishing line over my shoulder and the gun and knife bumping against my thighs in their leather holsters. The fire is hungrily burning the dry sticks she has collected.

I climb the bank and walk beneath the feathery shade of the leafless trees. The grill and frying pan are on the fire. The oil is getting hot. The two fish will sizzle themselves to perfection. The bush behind the camp is thorn-thicketed and pressed down by the ascending sun and the high power of the clear brilliance of sky. The insects are crackly through dry leaves and the early morning smells have left us for dryness, sucked away by the sheer power of sun. The river flows on behind me. That doesn't change. I'm hungry.

"Thanks for getting it ready. I couldn't have waited much longer."

"I'm hungry too. We'll have bacon and sausages after the fish, and coffee and toast and if that isn't enough I'll send you out with the big gun to bring in some meat."

"I'm sure the buffalo will be pleased if we find we're no longer hungry."

I lower the shot fish into the hot oil – water and oil explode against each other. The crackling continues happily until I drop the second fish into the big frying pan – and then the explosions begin again. It's a man-sized pan, this one. A rug, a fire, a fish, a woman.

"I'm glad Jim isn't coming back till late tomorrow, Stella – we can have all day to ourselves and then sneak back down the river just before dawn tomorrow. Life should always be like this."

"But it can't be."

"What do you mean? Don't sound so unhappy – it's been so different up till now. We'll get many days like this together – and they'll be all the better for looking forward to. It's been over a year now and no one but Max has found out and I couldn't care a stuff about him. We're just beginning to be happy. It's never been as good before – and usually with men and women it gets worse and not better. Come and give me a kiss and say 'hell' to the rest of the world. They don't care about us so why should we care about them?"

"But it's me, Guido, that I'm worried about. I tried to find out that night with Ted whether I was building fantasies in my mind about you. But I wasn't. Jim can go and sleep around and I don't care, but seeing you look at Berna in a way that told me you were thinking of more than sex made me almost sick with fear and hopelessness. I saw my life had come to an end that night and that making do with Jim wasn't enough. I know our relationship can only be made up of moments like these and I won't forget them in a hurry – but there must be someone in the world who can give me this kind of happiness permanently – and I'm going to have another look for him. If you don't feel something for someone then life is empty. I feel for you, Guido, but I can't go on 'feeling' for someone I pretend not to know when I meet him in company. You've shown me that feeling does exist and that the rest of life doesn't have to be put up with. Apart from our moments, life over the last few years hasn't even been worth the rub. Only in the last six months have I known what I was looking for... I'm leaving Jim and this valley and you too, Guido. The last is going to hurt for a long time... I've a favour to ask – it's the first and last we'll ever ask each other. I want you to drive me into Salisbury. From there I'm going to Durban and from there I'm going to look for a man I can feel for permanently. If he doesn't love me the same way it won't matter. I won't sleep around as I did in Paris. That side of me is over. I'll just be looking for him and when I get a bit down, as I will, I'll think of this valley and Guido Martelli. This is my only chance. I'll soon be getting too old to find a second chance."

"Haven't you thought how I'll feel about this? Haven't you thought I might want to marry you? How can you tell me now that you're just up and offing and all you want me to do is give you a ride into town? Haven't you realised what this has meant to me and what it means to me now?

I've never felt like I have done these last thirty-six hours and I'm a lot older than you – and I've been looking for this just as hard. If you'll divorce Jim I'll marry you, Stella, and to hell with Max Rosher and his consequences. You don't need money anymore. You've as good as told me."

"... Do you think we could marry?... Doesn't our feeling belong to places like these? No, we'd run out of love because what we have is too violent. We burn up too much too quickly. I think you love me in moments like these but I can't make you love me all the time. You want more than a sexual love – and having been so close to you I can tell... I didn't think you'd ever ask me to do what you have, but it doesn't matter anymore. At times it could have meant everything. I hoped this could have come out later, this afternoon, seeing you as you were – happy... My clothes are packed and I'm booked at the Windsor for the one night in Salisbury. If we get to the sugar estate at dusk no one will see us drive off. The train leaves for Durban at nine tomorrow morning and I'm going to be hard about it till then – so don't look at me like that. Ours is an affair, Guido, an affair – don't you understand? However perfect this is, there's nothing more than just this and this isn't a lifetime. As you say, you're older than me – you should see the ultimate emptiness more easily. You've got a job here and however much you like to discount it, you'll have to do something to make money and something else is sure to be worse. There is a lot of good for you here."

"There won't be much when you're sunning yourself on the beach at Durban. I could talk to Max into letting me stay here."

"And enjoy every moment afterwards knowing he'd got you completely under his thumb. You'd hate even yourself. The fish are burning. They need turning over."

"I haven't much stomach for food. They can bloody well burn. Just when you think you've got something worth having it crumbles away. Why won't you change your mind?"

"It wouldn't do us any good."

"There are more places than this to live in. Provided you have the right kind of person, the rest doesn't matter."

"You'd grow bored with me. You need a lot to keep you occupied. The bush is merely your relaxation. You need the rest as well."

"You're wrong, so wrong. I need the right woman and this. The rest can go to hell along with all the Max Roshers of the world."

"I'm sorry, Guido. I can't take the chance. I couldn't take life if it didn't work again, and however much my feeling yearns to say yes and stop thinking about all the problems of life, I can't. I can see how it would be... And so could you if you wanted to. I have learnt my lesson and it's time to put the knowledge into practice before it's too late. Stop it. Don't look like that. We came together in the first place because we both wanted sex and it's been like this for most of the time. I can't help it if it's suddenly become different. I've made up my mind and it mustn't be changed or there'll be nothing left of me in a couple of years."

"Do you really think you'll find what you want?"

"At least I'll try."

"Oh, grow up, Stella. That person doesn't exist for anyone. Life is just an existence. This hope of perfection, of permanent happiness, is really its most sought-after red herring."

"He must exist. I've seen it with other people."

"You think you've seen it. Anyone seeing us half an hour ago would have thought they saw it in us, and at that moment they would have been right, but look at us now. It'll mean that either Jim or I will have to leave the sugar estate but there are a few other places similar to this in Rhodesia where I can get a job and we can live together. It won't always be perfect and we'll argue like hell at times but I think there's a spirit between both of us which is strong enough to give us sufficient happiness to say that life is worth the struggle."

"And what about Berna? Didn't you think you loved her as well?"

"I thought I could love Berna but that was different to what I find here. Maybe with Berna it's her youth I envy, maybe it's something else, but so far I haven't found out and if you'll agree to stay with me I won't bother to solve the problem. You think you can find the perfect person but I don't think I can anymore. I'd like to, yes, but that's as far as practicability can let it go."

"I'm in too much of a mess. Let me go now. Let's see how we feel in a few months. That's the sensible thing to do, isn't it? Let me do a bit of searching and prove myself wrong."

"All right. I'll wait for you. Get your divorce going so we won't have to wait too long afterwards. Now, if the fish haven't burnt too much we'll eat... No, they're too bad. The side furthest from the flames will be the best burnt, there's usually one side better than the other in everything. We've got till four o'clock and that's a long time to enjoy ourselves as it may be a long time before we see the Big River again together, if I know my Max Rosher."

## 21

"Stop making so much of it. I won't be the first person to marry someone else's wife... You're talking too loud and the line can't take it... Yes, she's gone. Right now she's halfway to Durban... Oh come off it, Max, you told me yourself you knew all about it... Sure Jim thinks I'm a bastard but I didn't stop speaking to him after he slept with Elio... And from all reports he also got to my sister before you did... And don't you call her a whore whatever she might have done... No, the girls are still here and don't know anything more than that Stella's gone to Durban for a holiday... Sure they probably think, but thinking is one thing and knowing is another. ... Yes, they can chaperone each other. ... Yes, Max, I want to stay here when I'm married... You sure change your bloody mind when it suits you. You've been trying to get me married off for eighteen months and now I want to do it you're threatening to kick me out... Look, Max, if I want to marry her, you and your whole shit-happy little army aren't going to stop me. So get it into your head you either have both of us or none of us. Sure... sure, that's the kind of idea I expected from you – he'd make just about the finest arse of himself as managing director. When it comes to management, Jim couldn't organise a piss-up in a brewery... Fine, Max, now I know your sentiment... Oh, don't talk shit. For a while they'll talk and after three months something else will crop up to capture their interest. They'll forget Stella and me overnight and a year later that she was even married to Jim... You're not so lily-white yourself... Sure you didn't marry someone else's wife on the estate, but this has fallen to my prerogative. There's a first time for everything... You know something – you're a hypocrite... All right, I got the message earlier on. If I marry Stella, I get out of Gokwe Sugar Estates. Goodbye, Max, and sweet dreams."

The bastard. He's so low he's manure before he's dead. I just want to kick him in the crutch. He switches hot and cold with himself as his only interest. So now I know! And he'll make sure I don't get another job with a sugar company... We could go back to England and Harrogate Falls. No... that's one thing I couldn't live with. I just couldn't even start to fit in. There must be jobs in Salisbury. Oh, hell, I can't even be bothered to think about it. Let it all wait. I'll write it to Stella and between us we'll come up with a simple answer. There's always an answer to anything only some are more difficult to find than others.

"Kango! Bring me a beer."

The sun hasn't gone down – it's only three in the afternoon. He really looks after me, that man. And where would he go? The bush is as much to him as it is to me. And if I get a nice little management job in Salisbury I'll ruin his life as well as my own. Ten years is a lot of time to have a man like that around you. I'd be pretty lost without him even if I do have to admit that I'm sentimental. You don't just heave up your own life but everyone else's around. Poor old Jim – he took it really badly. He said he'd kill me so I won't go out shooting with him for a while in case he engineers an accident. The girls must be bored on their own. Typical of Max not to think about them until he has time. They're out of his way where he thinks they won't get into harm so he forgets the problem. At some time in the future they'll fit into his plans and he'll be all expansive and urgent and rush them to wherever they can do him some good. Anyway, the bush is still a novelty to Berna – and she still looks at me in the same way. Why did it have to be Stella? Probably because she was illegal and apparently unobtainable. I've always wanted what I shouldn't have.

"Thanks, Kango. It looks cold."

The beer tastes good anyway. You look for something and you find it only to discover you're about to destroy everything else. All the pieces are there but they don't fit together. And if I get bored with Stella, as she says I will, I won't have anything but too much age with which to start again, woman-wise or job-wise. No, surely I won't get bored with Stella. We fit together. We know what the troubles are like and will be able to avoid them… Beer drinking in the afternoon has a certain illicit satisfaction. I must do it more often. The sun soaks out the alcohol before there's a kickback. Or should I just bugger off and forget everybody and everything? Maybe the problem's too big. Singapore or South America? Something like that. Bury myself for another ten years. I'd be forty-five at the end of that little lot and one or two more burials would see me at the permanent one. Seems an easy way out – especially while I'm sitting here with a beer. Maybe I should think of some other way of solving this woman question. Or is it so big and important after all? Without it I could sit back here with the beer and smile at everything. There won't be any uncertainty or need – just peace as it should be. And yet I think of giving up all this just to plunge myself into the problem even deeper with no real certainty that I'll solve the question or find any peace inside of it all. I must be crazy.

## 22

"Kango! Get the two big guns and the twelve bore. We're going into the bundu. We want blankets, water, coffee, salt and the hunting knives. We'll shoot the rest of our food."

Sitting around for two weeks by myself waiting for something to happen that doesn't is quite enough. Life must be lived and it's time I got on with it again. I should be thankful for what I've got and be satisfied.

"Shall I put them in the Land Rover or the boat?"

"The Land Rover. We'll go into the thick bush around Mpata Gorge."

"That's a long way. I'll bring plenty of water and extra petrol. The chains and winch are still under the seats of the truck. I'll check the tool kit and the spare tyre. This is going to be good. We haven't been on a big trip for months. I'll go and tell my wives in the compound so when we move, people will know we're coming and will watch for the game and tell us where to look. The kraal will be pleased to see us down there. It's over a year since we saw that village. They'll have much for us to shoot as a year is a long time to have goats taken by the leopard and lion without anything being done about it. Shall we go today?"

"Yes. We'll make first camp when it gets dark. There's a waterhole and saltlick about fifty miles along the track. We'll shoot something to eat there all right."

"How long do we go for?"

"That depends. As long as we're needed. We'll come back as usual."

"Now you're the big baas, can you be away like that? Things will happen here on the sugar estate. The other baases will take advantage."

"You know, Kango, I don't really care. I just want to get down there for a few days and live again. I've been away from that part of the valley for too long and it hasn't done me any good. I'll get like Baas Rosher if I'm not careful and you wouldn't like that."

"The whole valley wouldn't like that. They were pleased here when you got the job as it meant there were many things the people on the estate could do which you understood and didn't mind about. But they've been thinking you've changed and are wondering if you'll stop the small game poaching and the people pretending sick for a few days to go and bring back the meat. They will be pleased to see you out in the bush as usual. They will work better for you. It is not so much the new money you give them that they want but the right to go on living and hunting as before and not having to be worried about the 'time' they hear so much about. Yes, it's nice to be going out into the bush and to be coming back as usual and not in time for something. I'll put in the fishing rods as we may get tired of meat."

"IF FATHER INSISTS on leaving me in the bush I may as well do something interesting. Berna has been peculiar for weeks and just sits in the sun by the pool all day long – she isn't much company and anyway she doesn't seem to mind if I go or not. She's talking about going back to Ireland. I think she's bored or something. I mean Father should have collected us by now. Mrs. Carter in town will put Berna up at night, so she'll be safe." Maralene had come to the house after she had phoned and asked if she could join us.

"Did you suggest she came as well?"

"Yes, but she didn't show any interest. She hasn't been the same since the petrol bomb attack. I suppose coming from a country where you read about robberies and knifings in the paper, it came as a shock and upset her more than me. It adds a bit of excitement to life I always think. Life's dull if it keeps going on as expected."

"I don't think your father would approve of us going off alone, even with Kango. I've been known to do things to women that he doesn't approve of."

"Berna says you don't like sex."

"Oh, does she? Well you can promise her she's wrong."

"I don't really care what Father does think. If he leaves me here like this week after week, he must expect me to go off and find something to do on my own. Anyway, I love the valley. I saw it as a child even before you. We spent a fortnight up here when I was eight. Father was making a survey to find the best site for the estate. You came up the year after. I remember them saying they'd found a hunter to shoot out the game, but I never thought he would take over from Daddy as boss – but here I am and here you are."

"Yes... I suppose you can look at it that way."

It will make Max violent – he'll never believe I haven't taken advantage of her. It'll do him good to be stabbed where it hurts most and just maybe that's the only place where it will hurt. For once he won't be in control of a situation; and after that garbage he gave me on the telephone last month he deserves a little in return. Am I being vindictive? Probably, yes, but it will do me some good to get my own back, after I've kicked him in the teeth I'll feel better about seeing him around. She seems genuine in her reason for going, and even if she isn't, my mind hasn't the energy to pinpoint the fallacy in her argument. And she is a woman and after she and Berna leave there will be little enough of that.

Stella seems a whole world away. A barrier of all the people between here and Durban seems to be between us. They have cut our bonds of communication. She is so far away that my instinct fears for her return. She could have met what she's really looking for. Probably she only agreed to come back to make the parting easier or more likely because she wanted to at the time. The new influences around her will be stronger than any of her ties from the past. If she finds an enjoyable social life, even without her ideal, she will be sufficiently satisfied to look back on us as a pleasant interlude, a part of her life she wouldn't have missed and which taught her she was right to leave Jim. She'll convince herself that that part of her life needn't be gone back to because going back to anything is bad and never the same as before.

If she comes back to me, because she has found unhappiness, we must consider it as a new venture and excitement and not as a consequence of our past. I must continue my life now as I am, alone, and only change it when there are two of us. I cannot live in the hopes of a planned future as life is not predictable. There are too many people in the world to influence us away from our instincts. She's had plenty of time to reply to my letters.

"If you come, Maralene, I won't be acting as host, chaperone, or guide. Kango and I are out for fresh air. You're welcome to follow us where we go. I'd enjoy having you along in that case."

"I don't care how I come as long as I get out of this place and do something."

"You'll need a mosquito net and sleeping bag. If you can find a camp bed you'll find it softer on your bones."

"A blanket under a tree is still good enough. Sleeping on a camp bed gets cold just before dawn. I prefer being right on the ground."

"Kango, go and get the .275 and look for some shells. I'll clean it out at the first camp.

"If Maralene knows about sleeping under trees, I presume Maralene knows how to use a rifle – you won't be bored if you have a gun of your own. Anyway, it'll give you something to defend yourself with. I'll drive you down to your father's house to get what you need and by the time we get back Kango will have loaded the truck... heh, Kango?"

"Sure, baas. We want to get going soon to be at that waterhole before dusk. If we get there afterwards we won't have anything to eat tonight."

The sun is still hot as we walk out of the stoep and onto the gravel path that runs parallel to the pool. I feel better now that I'm doing something I want to do. The estate can run itself for a few days. The hood of the car is folded back. She opens the passenger-side front door.

"Mind! The seats will be hot. There's a rug on the back seat for the purpose."

I lean in and get it. She takes it from me and spreads it across the plastic seat cover. She gets in and presses her hips up to move her bare thighs along without ruffling the rug and at the same time holds it in place with her shoulders. The apple-green shorts press her between her legs. I get in. The car starts with one turn of the engine and purrs in the warm air. We reverse and turn powerfully around the drive under the slight pressure of my right hand on the power steering. I slit my eyelids against the glare of the sun. The road drops from the high ground towards the softness of the green cane carpet below us.

The incline levels out and lets me press in the third gear and pedal some power. The dust line builds up behind us, too slow to settle back on anything but the road and dry, red-encrusted grass of the dry bush on either side. We move in fast between the cane rows and brush them swiftly on either side with the windscreen – we both duck and the rug slides off the back of the seat. I slow at the intersection and look right –

the sausage-like feed pipe of the irrigation system lies across the road. I accelerate on. Up ahead, water spurts onto the road and cane in its spluttering, powered circle. We duck again but the trajectory turns on us exactly. We laugh. A bucket of water has gone over each of us – Maralene's white blouse is opaque and sticks to the smooth tops of her breasts and the folds around her navel. She tries to pull it away, catches me looking and smiles into my eyes with an expression that tells me that's how it is and she hopes I like it. Put like that I do!

The next intersection is free of irrigation pipes to the right and takes us round to the far side of the big house, the acme of executive opulence. The car climbs the tarmac driveway and stops in front of the triple garage in oiled wood-panels from Mozambique. The terraced garden drops away on all sides from the two-storey house with its big sterile rooms.

"Go and talk to Berna while I get my things together. She's down by the swimming pool, I expect. I'll bring an umbrella for the return trip or do you like the new, skin-wet style?"

"It does a lot for you."

"I'll have to jump into the pool and make a good job if it."

She goes into the house. She'd look good with her hair clinging wetly to her face. She has one of those smooth-skinned, heart-shaped faces that look better without any frills.

The idea of Berna must have been the last twinges of a man getting old. I recognise it as such now. Life is for real. Seventeen years of sleeping around and feeling a lot sometimes only to find that 'life' destroys all the little utopias, and then struggling to tell myself there was one more who was what I wanted, who'd be perfect... and then one more... and then one more... and then on to thirty-five and teenagers' shirts clinging to them, should have made me realise that that's how it is before this. I must have too much of something that's no good for me but that's how I'm made. I can't change the pattern of life, however much it needs changing.

I walk away from the car across the hard tarmac to the path that leads down to the swimming pool. The flower beds are prolific, unlike mine at my house that look up with bare, sun-baked earth. But here, where they grow close together, the sun can't get in between the cannas and tangles of wisteria to suck out the underground moisture. The bougainvillea runs red and riots up the bush-timber poles that Max put up for them. In between the trellises, and a little down the slope, I am lost to the house. I am part of the forced colour of man-made garden, his little world of order. I yawn and that's a bad sign for anything. I walk softly on my rubber soles and make no noise with the sun and silence and the red dollops of flowers hanging from the trelliswork against the brilliant blue of the true Africa – the groomed animal in me is the groomed world of artificiality. I feel hemmed in and silently obscured. Small rocks border the path, chosen for their equal size. A run of water has spread new, red-wet earth from the hearts of the flowers that only live because they are regularly watered. I wonder if they know this fact. There are no weeds, only flowers in predestined lines and places. The bougainvillea creeps where it is told to creep and hangs where it can. Not even the bees have found this paradox strange. The ants make the best of an unaccustomed job and build up their hillocks under the green leaves and yellow flowers – the hoe or trowel will find them and then they will start all over again. The brightly coloured birds shun this garden for better places in the bush. The sun ignores the difference and so would the locusts if only they could get their chomping, wicked little jaws into such a perfumery. There are steps here – and now another path, exactly the same, down from the drop of two feet, winding round the hill to contour it so that all the pumped-on water doesn't rush off laughing to the bottom of the hill. I'm wrong. Over there, a green, black-striped lizard has made his home in the new world and seems to be enjoying his dominance and solitude. The pool is around this next bend, or so I remember. Looking back, I can just see the top of the house jutting its head up desperately to see over the slopes of its foundations. I shiver a little at the overpowering sight and the weight of its black-tiled roof.

 The glint of new water crystallises in the gap of trellis and creeper and its concrete corner grows bigger as I walk round and nearer and the flat, primed expanse of its sidewalk gives on to a small foot, a long calf, a firm sun-tanned thigh, a cleft of potential pleasure, and the round, rising rump of comfort, and up and over to a thickly fleshed spine and the firm shoulders and turned-away face. She is almost golden from the sun and shines ripely from her sun-tan oil. There is nothing artificial about this. Her body is as perfect as man could ever have made it. I stand in the open, just away from the entrance, and watch. She is probably asleep. I take off my shoes and walk to the pool and let myself down to the ledge of tiles and lower my corny feet below the water – too much bush walking makes them like this. Her face is now more towards me and the softness of her cheek and corn-ripe hair blend smoothly.

There isn't a blemish on the surface of her. The one-piece backless bathing costume is pure white. To look at she is perfect and there is only one way to satisfy this sight. It's what that is for and not to be thought about and conjured into something that dispenses all the needs for man. That, there, has the requisite to dispense one need and from it produce another – children. Anything found in addition is luck. The delicacies of society don't really exist when it comes to this and there isn't an aesthetic nature in man that looks at it in any other way – despite what I've hoped for in the past. It's merely just a pity that life isn't different to what it is – at least what it is now in the twentieth century.

The water's so warm my feet don't feel any contact. The sun is pressing on the back of my neck. She should be wearing a hat. Her eyelids flicker and show me a look of softness and inquisitiveness that comes to me unhurriedly across the water. The eyelids open a little more. The brown eyes looking up at my face seem to be pleased and, because of this, let the lids shut again. A smile imperceptibly comes over her face and stays there. She settles more comfortably onto the concrete and tile. The eyelids flicker and shut. The slightly open legs come together and the stage is set. I look out at the distant cane and even more distant bush and escapement hills... And back up at the trellised and terraced garden, at the hardness, the almost violence of the house. The bad feeling and taste comes back to me and a pain moves into the dip above the bridge of my nose. Thirty-five's a lot of years to be sitting like this. And nineteen years over there suggest a lot of heartbreaks ahead. The house looks permanent, more so than the hills that have held in the flow of the river for all of past serenity. But someone will find something of value inside of them to warrant blasting them open.

I take off my shirt and wristwatch and put them down beside me on the white tiles... And flop forward into the warm water and swim slowly towards the other side. The water feels strange in my shorts but the solace of coolness is worth the peculiar feeling. This isn't getting me into the bush but it is giving me some of the answers I was going to look for. I roll onto my back and let the fierce sun darken my sight and sustain my moment of freedom from everything. The world up there is blue at the edges. I float while the world hangs still and the sun holds its own with the afternoon. I don't think or care whether worlds exist or that life is me or that anything is really needed apart from what I've got. I float – there's nothing but me – the pool is soft. My eyes see less as the sun powers itself into their sockets. I could stay here content, in a world that is only mine.

I splash hard to get my head above water and wonder quickly if I would have drowned if I'd let the inertia of my mind continue to control my body. I move into the crawl and power myself towards the other end, feeling the pressure of water building up under my chin and against my shoulders. I touch the edge and let my forward movement push me out and turn me round to sit where I was before. She hasn't moved. I stand up, and, dripping away from my watch, walk round to her. I put one knee on the tiles beside her having made up my mind. I smooth my hand gently down her back and over the soft mound and then back slowly to her neck. Her legs go slightly apart on the third run and let my hand feel the inside of her thigh. I doubt if she is a virgin after all. She pulls her face round and looks up at me. Her eyes say yes – her lips are firm and thick to touch and her mouth and tongue are strong. We come apart to breathe.

"Not now, Guido, Maralene may come. Spend the evening with us and then afterwards we'll be alone."

"You seem to have had experience."

"None at all. I told you that last time and it put you off."

"It wasn't that. I was trying to join too many feelings together – and it isn't possible. I should have agreed with you last time. You've taught me something, Berna."

"I just lay here and waited for you to come across. I could feel that you would."

"Come for a swim."

"Pick me up and carry me down the steps into the pool. I want you to put me in the water."

"I was going into the bush but it can wait till tomorrow."

"It'll be nice having dinner with you. You feel strong."


SHE HAS on a young girl's dress that is full of colour and flares from her waist to just above her knees. Her breasts are too large to be modest and bulge smoothly and roundly above the straight-line cut of her top. Maralene looks pretty in a white dress and I feel old enough to have fathered them both but I don't think this comes into it. Kango wasn't pleased when I postponed our trip till tomorrow morning. Here there are only the three of us. They each look as clean and unspoilt as the other. Their freshness is youth. Berna's perfume is lily-of-the-valley and Maralene's is lavender. A cry from my youth and the old animal brought me here. Most men are unfaithful. The act means little more to them than what it physically expresses. In many countries men live with more than one wife and everyone gets along very well together. It's better to overcome any feeling I have for her now so I won't look back and blame my bad future for not having done something at the time. This can be true for her as well as for me. If there isn't anything afterwards, then it won't matter anymore. I've stopped trying to conjure these things.

Max's big dining room glistens with silver and polish. The three set places are spacious in their separation and would be cold and sterile without the long, fat candle burning up evenly between salt cellars and butter dishes. The wine glasses are clean and full of crystal-clear reflections. My stomach feels better for having drunk the three dry martinis outside on the veranda. The cook has on one of those ridiculous red fezzes that remind me of the Egyptian wars my father was too young to remember. I help Berna into her chair, then pour Hock into her glass and then Maralene's. They both had three cocktails which they were not used to. I fill my own glass to the brim and sit down for the food. I am at the top of the table with the women on either side, with the young perfumes to go with the just-greying hair at my temples. I converse and interplay with words and get on with the oldest game of life – I'm playing it by ear – the benefits of age! Berna lacks nothing for making a man want her – there's not a thing wrong. The hair falls to below her ears and parts itself softly in the middle of her forehead. The brown eyes are big and soft above the rich, sun-tanned skin. Her mouth is smooth with coral lipstick and her eyelids have been touched with blue that rides like the glistening, velvet night in the flicker of the candle's flame. Her soft arms lead down to soft, short-fingered hands – the nails are varnished with the colour of coral. Her legs need no stockings to produce a sensual colour – the sun has done that.

The food lands in front of us and words go out into the candlelight. She sits away from me, untouched and yet I feel the sex in the smallest movement of her body and eyes. The feeling conquers the taste of food and alcohol and evaporates the conscience of my upbringing and the 'don't touch it will break' of our past together. The crickets screech outside the gauzed windows. Frogs croak from the pool halfway down the terraces where the lizard keeps his lonely court. The flame flickers and plays shadows into the faces of the other two diners and Hockdrinkers. She raises her glass to me and drinks silently and to cover my impulse I drink to Maralene as well.

The food plates go away and coffee comes forward to temper desire. Food is not so important as drink. Maralene empties her glass. I get up for the second bottle on the sideboard.

"I'll be jealous if I stay any longer, Guido. I'll tell the cook to go. Berna knows where the gramophone is if you want anything like that. I'm glad you came to dinner with us. I was getting bored at the sugar estate until tonight. I hope you two turn out all right."

We say the necessary good-nights and then find ourselves alone. There is enough alcohol in both of us to prevent any words. I go over to the sideboard and de-cork the second bottle and fill up her glass. She looks up so I kiss her for no better reason than I want to. I go back to my chair and sit down and drink and stare across at her, hiding nothing of my thoughts. Our eyes communicate. The wine is dry and cleans my palate. Her scent is powerful. Her breasts rise and fall with her breathing. The silk of her dress clings to them as it does to her waist.

"Let's get out of this room, Berna. It doesn't belong to us."

"I'll lead the way."

Her voice is constricted with need. The saps go rising inside of me.

She gets up and I follow her past the length of the table and out into the lounge that has a full moon to light it and nothing else – I could read a book by its light. She goes up the stairs, bringing her index finger to her mouth. We go up as conspirators, one behind the other.

The moon doesn't penetrate at the top of the stairs along the corridor that leads off into the bedrooms. The first has a light under the door that we go past silently on the thick pile of the corridor carpet. She opens the last door but one on the left and I follow her in. The moon shines into her room without colour. I put the Hock bottle and our half-full glasses on the windowsill. The moon reflects in a sliver of the pool and grows larger as I lean out further. She comes next to me. Our lips touch. I run my hand over the soft silk of her shoulder. I fill our glasses and raise mine to the moon and then to the valley and river out there. I want to savour the feeling that grips me for her – there is a limit to being able to savour. I put down my glass and hers and pull her round. Our bodies press into each other and our mouths move together. The pressure increases. My fingers find the metal tag of her zip and pull it down. She eases away from me slowly and lets my hands part the material from her shoulders so it falls to her waist and the moon catches the whiteness of her bra. She moves just away from me and pushes the dress down over her hips. The alcohol has removed any fear she should have if this is to be the first time. The little drink in me is enough to tell me it doesn't matter what I take – if I don't, someone else will, and she offers too much not to be accepted. I lift her onto the bed.

## 23

It is totally dark. The moon has gone but the day-birds haven't yet woken. They will soon feel the pressure on their instincts to get up and ruffle their feathers before welcoming the new day. Her body is naked and firm against mine. She sleeps without sound. My eyelids are heavy from too little sleep and my mouth feels the remnants of gin and German Hock. There is a soft feeling in my belly of satisfaction. I must go before the house wakes. What Maralene suspects must be different to what she knows. I think she knew last night but it mustn't be me who precipitates the truth. Berna's ear is soft as I kiss and nuzzle some reaction from her. She wakes slowly, as though from a deep and good sleep. I find her mouth and kiss it gently. I feel over her stomach with familiarity – the skin is pure, heavy, silky.

"I must go, little one. The light will come up in the sky in half an hour."

"I don't want to wake up. It's nice here."

"Do you feel good?"

"Lovely. Put your arm around me."

"Come into the bush with me. Maralene will understand."

"I'd like that. We can be alone for a long time. Kiss me and I'll get up with you. No one needs to see us go."

Out there it won't matter what the hell other people think on the estate. It is rare that evenings progress so well. I would spoil last night if I made love to her again – the first time together should be savoured to the full and future fulfilment kept waiting as long as possible.

I half throw back the one sheet and get out of the single bed that has only been supporting half of my body, and rummage with my feet on the dark floor for some clothing. I have no wish to turn on the light, but wait for the birds and the new dawn to show me the way. The air is fresh and newly cleaned by the darkness. I think they are my pants. Yes, the slit confirms such hopes and is borne out by the lack of silk I remember so well from last night. I collect the other garments and fumble myself into them one after the other. The bed creaks as she sits up. She slides off the bed and stands up. The silhouette gives me a strong urge to go back to bed that is difficult to overcome. She gropes to the built-in cupboard across from her side of the bed, opens it and pulls things out and begins to get dressed. There is still no light in the east but a bird, seemingly in the calm, cool valley, has cleared its throat, either as a prelude to a dawn chorus or as a part of his dream. The cool air comes up to me here in fresh waves of newness and removes any semblance of age from my bones. I was born today and the newness of my realisation is exciting and pumping with the pleasure of life.

"You'll need shorts, underclothes, flat shoes and a hat. The rest Kango has put in the Land Rover."

"I think I'm ready and if I'm not it doesn't matter. I'll wash when we've sneaked round to your house."

"We can push the Chev and run it backwards down the hill without using the engine. That way we'll be gone without sound or trace."

"Maralene will know where we've gone. She suggested I might like to go instead of her yesterday."

"I think there's some conspiracy."

"There needed to be the two of us with you – I'm afraid Maralene caught a little of the fever while she was trying to help."

"Do all girls scheme like that?"

"No, as most girls don't know what they want."

"You can give me a kiss for that... Umm... That's just nice."

"Let's go. You lead the way."

THERE IS no need to talk. The Land Rover bumps us along, side by side in the cab, the engine driving us deeper and deeper into the bush. The trees are shorter here and the patches of sand more frequent. My firm grip of the black-taped wheel is familiar and friendly. My mind jumps back to her regularly as it has done since we left the sugar estate this morning. We are not sitting close to each other as it would be too hot – the windows are half shut and tsetse fly gauze covers what gap there is. Kango is behind the truck part, balancing himself and a .375 on the extra full drum of petrol. The flies take no notice of him, or maybe it's the other way round.

The bush is very dry. It hasn't rained for five months. We shall see game nearer the river. There isn't a waterhole for thirty miles and even that may be dried up by the parched look of everything. The trees are stark and thorny. The grass has been trampled and eaten long months ago by the herds of buffalo, kudu and zebra. Here and there are torn trees where elephants have ripped the bark from the saplings to eat – some of the older and heavier trees have been busted by too much use as back-scratchers. The tsetse buzz persistently but everything else except us is still and quiet under the heat of the sun that silences everything. The track was made by elephant. This has been my road into the wilderness for years and I still use a compass to check my bearings. There are few landmarks in the bush – the ones that are change with the bush fires. The big rock outcrops remain but they look different after a fire. The permanent way is the elephant way, punctuated by dung heaps in cylindrical mounds the size of a bucket, and pounded by the flat, often spoor-less pads except for the toes of the seven-tonne mammals. I have shot nine elephant, because they consistently made floor coverings with the growing cane, but each time I have been conscious of their deaths for days afterwards. We are their only enemy. They ride through the bush of Africa, oblivious of other animals except as something that feeds or drinks at a distance or more often runs away. A lion would be rolled on if it had the stupidity to attack, which it rarely has.

WE ENTERED the flat plain that is the river five minutes ago and the *vlei* is studded by the deep, sun-baked holes of the animals. In the rains this plain becomes marsh and the buffalo sink in up to their knees. The sun has lost some of its heat to the evening. If I stop the truck I will smell the river. I can see Kango's legs through the slit of Perspex when I half turn round. He is balanced across the cab roof trying to get us something for the evening meal now we are close to the river. It is too early for the big herds to have come down to drink. They wait in the thorn scrub till dusk.

Far over to our left is a small kraal. We will go there tomorrow and hear the local gossip. It is the only one for twenty miles up or down the river – the thatch-topped houses are built on stilts as a precaution against leopard and buffalo. They herd a scrubby variety of goat, which are immune to the tsetse fly, and grow millet despite the game. The government has legislated the need for licences to kill the game but I'm sure the gentlemen over there eat as much fresh meat as they can catch, and will go on doing so provided they don't commercialise their butchery. There are trees far out in front of us along the banks of the river, but here it is scrub.

"I'm looking forward to you throwing buckets of water over me."

"Another ten minutes will see us there."

The rifle cracks again over my head and makes me swerve and hope that this time he has shot something. The pounding on the metal roof above my head makes me stab the brakes and bring the twenty mph down to nothing. Kango leaps out with the rifle and runs towards a thicket some thirty yards off and behind us, taking no notice of the hoof holes and tufts of grass. He reaches the bushes and carefully puts his hand in, trying, no doubt unsuccessfully, to avoid the thorns, and pulls out a dead buck, weighing, I'd say at this distance, some thirty pounds. It's good shooting from a rolling, jerking truck. He drags it towards us over the scrub and heaves it into the back, climbs in himself, and we move on to the river. I put my hand gently on her bare thigh as I know what she's thinking.

It is dark looking out across the river. My rifle is within reach and close to the fire, spluttering under the fat from the spitted buck. Behind, the sky is blood-red between the gaps of trunks to just above the silhouettes of the trees. The crickets are violent, grinding away with their wings – the screech section of the bush orchestra. Kango has gone off with the spotlight to see if he can shoot a crocodile. I should have gone with him, but I can't please everyone – and at the moment I can think of nothing better than having my back to a big tree, a beer in my left hand, Berna propped into my lap, and my right hand resting lightly on her. Kango must have seen the look in my eyes when he suggested the 'off' half an hour ago.

With my left foot I turn the spit handle while my right moves easily in between hers. Between sips of our beers, and hers has a dash of lime juice straight into the bottle, we kiss and I'm quite sure I haven't left school but don't care. Our bed is set out behind the fire and the big blanket rests lightly on the dry grass Kango and I collected when we first arrived. It is enticing but must be fought against. These perfect pleasures must be spaced out and accentuated. Here is quite enough for the moment and here is perfect as it can't be satisfied.

I twist the spit a little more with my left foot and cant the stuck-up feet to a more precarious angle. I bring my right foot up gently but firmly between hers and then slide it down again with considerable pleasures to the left which she returns. Satisfied for a moment, I suck at the neck of my beer bottle and draw in more air than beer, tip harder, drain it and put it down with the other empties and pick up a full one, put the bottle against my left thigh, catch the lever under the top, and press up, using one hand only, as the other is better occupied. The froth bubbles gently out of the bottle as I bring it up to my mouth.

A splash that could be anything comes up to us from the river. It is no concern of ours. We all have our occupations. A distant shot tells me that Kango is winning himself some money as crocodile bellies fetch thirty pounds each.

This is a lost part of the world. In the dry season the river yawns its way down to the distant sea. The only way of getting here during the rains is by parachute and there is no guarantee of not joining the river in its rush to the sea. There is game in profusion and little else.

Another shot. Kango must have walked a long way. I turn the spit again and the buck over-balances and thrusts its dead feet down at the flames. I sniff the surge of cooking meat and lace the water in my mouth with a little beer. I feed her a little from my beer bottle and move back an inch on the bark of the tree and drink myself. I put my hand inside her bra.

There is a shallow, white glow above where the sun went down and I can see by turning my head and looking beyond the gnarled, harsh bark of the tree an inch and a half from my left eye. This tree is pretty tall – kind of thing one likes to get under in circumstances like these. I would like to pick her up and run around with her for no reason whatsoever. Stella! Why do I suddenly think of her when there's no need?... Yes. I picked her up and ran into the river and how little time ago it was and she's had time to write, but hasn't, and neither have I. If she comes back now what do I say? That you didn't write so I've changed my mind and found something else in the meantime to pass my time with? 'Poor

Stella', because there is nothing I can do about you now and if you come back without having found your own need, I won't be able to explain what has happened to me? I can say the language isn't good enough but this won't convey anything unless you know how I feel. It's a long time to have waited but worth it – worth all the feelings of worthlessness. This 'now' is enough for the past and future. I half want more but it won't matter. I've found a little bit of perfection in my life at last.

The gun again from the dark. The flow of water in front – and the bush around. I am feeling to the ultimate. The knowledge of existence is here with its reason.

## 24

"Was it you shooting last night? When Kango came back with a clean barrel you had us worried. My name's Guido and this is Berna. Do you want a beer or is it too early in the morning?"

"Thanks, I'll have one. Martin Crouper from Johannesburg. This is a friend of mine, Johnny Listworth from Salisbury. We're both in the travel business. They said no one comes in here."

"I thought the same."

"And I didn't expect to see anything quite like your wife so far off the beaten track."

"She's not my wife."

I take her hand and hold it while Kango hands out the beers and keeps one for himself.

"Do you want to join us for breakfast? We're having bream."

"Thanks. The river makes me hungry. I could eat anything just now."

What else could I say? She'll be here when they've gone.

The terms of my life are now apparent to me. This is my full understanding of existence. I am at peace all the way through myself – both my brain and body are calm. So many of the coils and sinews have gone and will never get into me again, not because I will always be happy, as this can never be true, but because I will see life for what it has been worth. I will be able to look back from my old age and prelude to death and know that it was worth all the other things. I will be mellow in my death. There will be no bitterness or flashes of frustration. There will be an acceptance of my fate and hope for the future generations of me through my children. For this feeling of wholeness I have had all the other pain and uselessness or normal, carnal life, of material life. Nothing can destroy this in me now because it will lodge in my memory for all of my existence however long or short that may prove to be. All this river and bush and people are the stage for this realisation. The hope for humanity exists in the intangible, unearthly feeling that flows un-engineered between her and me. So much for the world of materialistic civilisation – it has found nothing to justify its existence. Isn't life justified by love, whether like this or for God or for mankind? – a pure, untempered un-manmade love of feeling outside of our selfish needs. This feeling I have for her is the only unselfish act in my life, as the rest have had motives.

"Do you know these parts well? It's the first time Johnny and I have got this far into the bush. We came to see if money can be made out of a place like this with a bit of advertising."

"What are you going to advertise? Most people have heard of the Zambezi and there are easier ways of getting to it than here."

"No, it's the game. Here you can shoot it with a permit. We want to unload some of the rich men's money right here in this part of the valley."

"Sure, and we've big ideas to really get at the heart of their money. It was Martin's idea, but as he doesn't know Rhodesia so he came to me for advice and a partnership. I've been running safaris here on and off for six years but never in a big way. The big way makes the big money. You've got to invest to draw out the golden tooth and there are plenty of these in Europe and America, and not a few in the Republic. The boys in Jo'burg have been coining it these last five years and they're no longer frightened to offload as they can see there's plenty more where the first lot came from. But you've got to do it right to get at the rich. They want to appear as though they're roughing it so they can show the film slides and bore their friends at home, but in fact they want all the comforts and above all they want ice – you've got to give a rich man ice in his drinks even if you've parked him right here."

"Would you like some coffee first? The fish need cooking a little more."

"Thanks, Berna. Coffee on top of beer should be all right. Smells good. And that's another thing. The coffee must be from beans crushed just before brewing. These guys we're after are used to the right tastes and they've reached the stage in their lives where they don't want to change – anything – even here, and here is just about as far as you can get from anywhere. Now, this is how we have it. You see that rise way over there? It sits pretty high above that bend in the river and we've looked at it pretty closely and the river hasn't risen one third of the way up its hill even with five flood gates open eight miles up the river at Kariba. It's always dry as a bone on the top... And solid. That hill's rock – the perfect foundation. Martin and I are going to build a hotel up on top of that hill. It'll have just about the only windows in the world that will look out onto virgin plains covered in grazing, wild game. It'll look pastoral – but inside all of them as they watch they'll know that out there from their bedroom windows, out there from the glass circling the cocktail bar are the last true wilds, the last of nature as she's always been, and they'll feel big and rich for seeing it – and they'll know they'll have a gun in their hands next day to go out and satisfy their power in that wild country. They'll pay any money to see that from safety. They'll be unique amongst their friends. To be unique in this world costs big money. Government needs foreign exchange like every other country and this money that comes into our pockets will be just that. This is Crown Land but they've agreed to give a ninety-nine-year lease on enough of it for our hotel. We'll grade the road for two hundred miles to the tar to make the drive smooth, and later, out of profits, we'll put down a strip and bring in twin-engined Barons – so everything still looks safe and secure – none of this single-engined stuff. Think if it then – eleven hours from London, eighteen hours from New York, into the charter plane and three hours flying over thick bush brings them here, up there, in fact, on top of that hill with air conditioning... And ice in their drinks. This place is unique. We'll make a fortune opening it up."

"How big will you make your hotel?"

"Big enough to make it rich, but small enough to keep it exclusive. We want to be able to turn down six out of seven applicants and as the demand gets bigger, put up the price. That extra money will be profit."

"I can see you've thought of everything."

"You say that as though you don't like the idea. What's the use of all this unless it's put to making money for the country?"

"When you've been in the valley ten years by yourself and then someone says they're going to change it into a tourist empire, you have this kind of feeling and the face that goes with it."

"Do you know the river well?"

"Kango and I have become friendly with every waterhole and saltlick for fifty square miles on this side of the river. During the days of Federation we crossed over to the other side, but not anymore."

"But you're just the guy we're looking for."

"I don't think I am, Mr. Crouper."

"Sure you are. We need a white hunter to show our guests around. There's big money in it. These will be rich guys you'll be getting friendly with and rich guys give big tips for big service. There was a hunter I heard about in Kenya who got two thousand pounds' worth of guns at the end of a three-week safari – the guy didn't think he'd have time to do the trip again, and anyway he'd seen the place and once was enough to talk about. He liked the hunter. Just like that."

"I have a good gun that cost me seventy-five pounds and I wouldn't change it for anything – it trusts me and we've been friends for many years."

"Sure, but you sell the other guys' guns. Don't you see, you make two thousand pounds for the price of three weeks' pleasure."

"For me it would not be pleasure. Why don't you put in a casino like they're doing at the Victoria Falls? They could watch the game, suck at the ice in their drinks and watch the roulette wheel going round at the same time."

"How about that for an idea, Martin? I reckon if the government gave a licence to that guy up at the Falls, they'd give one to us. It'd be the same river that both lots of gamblers would be looking at. You've got good ideas, Guido. Maybe we should cut him in as a junior partner. He's got everything that's needed to run this end including business sense. A casino! Well, how about that? That takes the whole thing one big leap further forward. How come you've got a name like Guido? You sound more English to me than Italian."

"I was born in Italy. I worked on the dam at Kariba."

"Funny that. We had our eye on an Italian two years back when we first thought of the idea. You need the right manager and white hunter or this whole thing can fall apart at the seams. This guy knew the whole valley better than anyone else and they said he was the best white tracker and shot in Rhodesia – worked with an African, but only shot for meat and protection. At that stage we didn't have the financial backing so we couldn't approach him and make him an offer. If my memory is right his name was also Guido. He was working as a mechanic or something up at the big sugar estate and then out of the blue they made him general manager. It showed us we had our eye on the right man but that's just how business goes. I think you'd maybe fit into his place."

"Was his name Guido Martelli?"

"Yes, that was the guy. I remember his name sounded something like a trade name for brandy. You know him?"

"I am him, Mr. Crouper."

"That explains how you know all the waterholes and saltlicks."

"Yes, it does."

"There wasn't much likelihood of two guys knowing the same valley like that."

"I don't know of anyone else."

"We'll have to import a hunter and give him time to get to know the Zambezi Valley."

"You could do that."

"There are plenty out of work from Kenya and Tanganyika. Pity, we'll have to pay his passage and waste some time paying him without any profit. Sure you wouldn't like the job? I hear that fellow Rosher is a bastard to work for; if you'll excuse my language."

"Yes, he is."

"He's always in the papers spouting about something."

"He always talks a lot."

"Do you like the job?"

"No."

"Well then, why not change it to being in the valley working at your hobby?"

"It wouldn't be working at my hobby but destroying it."

"You wouldn't shoot much."

"The valley as I know it would have gone with the coming of your hotel. There would be no pleasure in it for myself – only a sadness."

"You must be one of those sentimental guys."

"Yes."

"Is the fish ready? Don't look so sad, Guido."

"That's right. The worst may never happen."

"It will."

So much has crumbled but that is life – my life anyway. There is no point in holding on to the valley as it will be gone soon and I'll be washed up by the river like so much flotsam, or float on, dead, down to the sea. It was fifteen months ago that I only had the problem of women. Now, there doesn't seem very much left in my life to ever support my problems. The world has caught up with me from all sides. There is just this little time left for me and after that there is a future the pain in my stomach won't let me contemplate. For this short time I sit under the pale fingers of the moon that may be reflected in my eyes and that anyway shine on the river. I can hear the voices of their tourists, even though they haven't come yet. The click of a spinning roulette ball and the dull calls of the croupier are loud in my ears. At thirty-five it is an effort to start all over again, especially when I know that the future of my way of life can never be as good as the past. But I mustn't lose her. I mustn't be foolish and let her go away as part of my despair.

Sitting next to me she feels my sadness but I don't think she understands it – why should she? She hasn't felt for this place like I have. And Kango, down there by the water's edge, will go on in it as best he can. I'll suggest to him he works for the commercial hunter who'll be taking over this part of the valley. The point has come where fighting the problem with my mind no longer has any point. I can't win. I accept this now. There is no outside path anymore. There are no longer any places in the world to run away to. The day of the conformist is here to stay for everyone. The outsider is dead.

"Let's walk down to the river."

"Why are you so sad? You were happy till those people told you about their hotel. What difference can it make?"

"None, really, except that it told me finally, and finally convinced me, that all this out here is at an end and that there is no point in hoping otherwise. I have accepted this now but it has hurt me even more than I can tell you. It has cut me in half, if that is understandable, seeing I am still walking and talking."

Automatically I bend down for the revolver and straighten up with effort and push it into my belt in front of my stomach. Everything seems the same, but it isn't the same at all. There is only nostalgia. The smells and sounds only help to tear at the dull, hard pain in the centre of my gut. My love for her is engulfed by this feeling. With luck, some of the pain will go away and the feeling I have for her will suppress and hold back the memories. I try to divert my thoughts to her as a woman but even this old trick doesn't work anymore. Nothing seems to be working anymore. The river flows, that is true, and the water must go on running down to the sea, but for the rest it will be torn apart, piece by piece.

I have so much to say to her, but the feelings in me are in contrast to any of the words. I feel for the words I want to tell her but this other pain is too much to let them out. The sand is still warm under my bare feet but I have no sympathy with it for the moment. Too much has crumbled. A whole life, picked up and shattered because it was never really there – an African summer – a summer of the bitter ending because here is no autumn or even winter afterwards. There is nothing. No, I am wrong. There is something. There is this hard pain in my gut.

We stop by the water, flowing inches from our toes. Kango is upstream behind the rock outcrop. I think he must be night-fishing he's been there so long. Or does he feel like me? Poor Kango. Poor Guido. Poor Mark. Three lives in an angry world.

She pulls me round to her and looks up into my face. My mouth comes slowly, almost painfully, down to hers – the pain, slowly, slowly, seeps out of my belly. A pulse tries to run in my blood. I draw her close to me and desperately squeeze. I hold my breath to capture this final moment of both worlds joined together. A little joy comes into my thoughts, as if the new world is taking over from my past. Only our mouths come apart and our eyes search for each other in the pale of the moon.

"Will you marry me, Berna?"

"You mustn't be serious about things. You make everything so important. I'm only nineteen. I hadn't really thought about marriage. I came out with Maralene to find love and passion – and I did. I wanted some experience before I started my first season in London."

We come apart but there is nothing for me to say. Not anymore.

"Daddy promised to give me one season and even though we won't actually be presented to the Queen, it's all great fun and I like that kind of fun. I'll have lots to tell them – all about Africa and white hunters and about real love down by the most exciting river that anyone ever saw. I think I'll be quite popular with the men and meet all the right people and then, after that, I'll think about marriage. Anyway, Daddy would never let me live out here, and till I'm twenty-one I have to do as he says. He'd never approve of my marrying an Italian in the wilds of uncertain Africa. He'd say there wasn't enough security in a marriage like that and though I'd love to go on living my life as romantically as this, even I know it can't last."

"I'm not a foreigner."

"Maralene said something about that but I didn't want to believe her as everything wouldn't have been so romantic. And the night of the petrol bomb wasn't real. I thought you just said all that. I mean no one else knew about it."

"Gordon Harrogate is my father."

"But everyone says he's just too rich and there wouldn't have been much point in you coming out here if that had been the case. That's why I didn't believe Maralene's stories and yours. Are you really his son?"

"Yes."

"He must have cut you off."

"On the contrary, he offered me the whole of Harrogate Falls. That's why he came out last month."

"Maybe we could do the season together."

"I'm too old for that."

"Yes, I wonder if Mummy or Daddy will mind about that? If I tell them you're very rich as well as very handsome I expect they'll overlook it. I hope you went to a good public school."

"Yes, I did that as well."

"Let me think about it. Marriage is a big step, you know."

"Yes."

"I don't think they'll mind about you being married before as divorce is so common in society these days."

"Who are 'they'?"

"Mummy and Daddy, of course."

## 25

"You must be loose in the nut," Max yells into my face. "One minute you're howling at me down the telephone about someone else's wife and a month later you're going to run off across the world after a teenager. Grow up, Guido, for God's sake grow up. You know as well as I do that you'd die like a fish out of water if you left this valley. You've both become part of each other. You thrive alongside this river. Look, things are going to be tough here with all this political nonsense but in the end politics sort themselves out and economics take over again. There isn't anything to run away from."

"I'm not running away from anything, Max. It's just that I have realised that what I came here for is about to disappear for all time and the only other thing left is Berna. If I have to change back to my old way of life then I will do – I can't afford to lose everything."

"You're talking a lot of rubbish. What the hell made me jump up a bloody electrician to managing director? I must have been crazy."

"I told you that at the time – if you remember I wasn't exactly overjoyed by the job."

"You're wasting your time with that girl. She's too young and stupid and will probably change her mind. You, in England! The very thought makes me laugh. There's plenty of crutch in the world without going six thousand miles to find it."

"You're pure filth."

"You asked for it, Martelli."

"No, not like that, Max, never swing a punch; it's too easy to stop. I told you once before you were too old for a roughhouse."

"You bastard."

"You wanted to fight, but as you can see it proves nothing. You may now run your sugar estate by yourself. Goodbye, Max."

The blood is oozing gently and satisfyingly out of the right-hand corner of his mouth and onto his well-cut suit as I leave my office and refrain from slamming the door. Kango can collect whatever I need.

I walk out into the sun. No matter where the road leads, to good or bad, there is now only one way to travel.

## 26

My stone kisses the smooth surface of the water and jumps back into the air and shoots on till its forward power goes and it sinks into the middle of the river to be below the water forever. The disappearance is quite final. The small birds will survive because they have no commercial value and can feed in among civilised gardens and fields as well as they can in the bush. The larger birds will be eaten for food like the animals – not now, of course, but in a nearer future than even I can suspect. I am right to leave all this. It is better to remember someone in health than sickness. I shall always have the memories. At first my children will listen... But they will soon grow impatient of me as my picture of my Africa will not agree with theirs that they will see on the cinema screen. There may be the spectacle but never the feeling because this type of feeling will have been lost to man. There will be no comparison. The metal, the concrete and the celluloid will have all the victories and the air will be cleaned by machines.

This is my farewell to the old world. My farewell to truth and nature. I only tried to fool myself that this would all last long enough for me and that I could bring a woman here and make a permanence. They were dreams – now shattered – now floating away with the evening flow of flotsam, of torn trees and weed and refuse – all discarded and unwanted.

The river is exactly as it was when I first watched its flow and saw the setting sun reflected in its surface. That fish eagle may be a relation of the first one that shrieked above the big water and made me grip my gun in fear. I listen to it now, relaxed. The gun is still with me as it is necessary but soon that will change... And I have no wish to see it. I crouch onto my haunches, dip my right hand into the sand and lift it and let the grains run through my fingers to show me the way of the world. There will be no need for such things in my future.

I haven't yet told Kango I'm going. He showed me all this in hours and days of walking. What freedom! There was nothing but us then. No worries. Everything was around us to be taken, and everywhere was our camp. There was no course set for us and no time to observe. There were no words, no human cruelty, no modern life. Out here, now, I am still free, but this is the last day, the last few moments.

A banana plantation would exist for a few years and then the tentacles of society would again reach the outsider and draw him back into the system to prove conclusively that the system of survival is right... And that there is no other way... Especially no better way.

There is freedom in love and feeling this, in the new world, can only be expressed between two people because it has not yet been possible to crush this instinct. Upon this I will base what is left of my life; and upon the memory of all this which enabled me to withdraw and understand a little of the roots of myself. It is necessary to eat and the one way this can be done is to earn a living, and the living from Max – or safaris or Harrogate Falls – is all the same and there is no alternative. Any that appear are merely procrastinations. I have reached an age where I must rejoin the system so as not to ultimately starve... And this factor becomes important with marriage and children and both of these are essentials for me to compete with the rest of my life. In the heart of a family there will be a little peace.

I am sad, yes, but mainly numb. The pain of realising I must leave has been so acute that it has now sapped all the energy from me. I should have driven off and not come down to the river but it is a part of us all that we wish to say goodbye – even to the dead when they no longer hear us. I think I will always have a pain ready to wake at this memory of what is here in front of and around me – but this must be seen as a small price for the peace of ten years. There will be other, smaller futures and these will be enjoyed in their time – they must be.

The sun is about to go down behind the escarpment hill. The hills are corn-yellow on the trees and grass and red on the rock and earth. The crickets zing and soon the hippo will come out of the water to graze and the crocs will watch for their food. It will go on like this for a little while.

She said she would not meet the plane at London Airport. I must buy myself a coat in Salisbury to keep in a little of the warmth. The Chev is waiting for me to drive into Salisbury so I can catch the aircraft tomorrow. They have agreed I can leave it for them to collect at the airport. I wrote this to Stella ten days ago but still no reply. I hope she has found what she wants. Jim is still on the estate and will stay there now. There is no reason for him to go. I haven't been able to see Ted. He will hear of my going – he will smile to think he never did catch me poaching. Maralene said she was going to take a flat in Salisbury and I expect she has done this by now. Father's cable showed me he was pleased. He has phoned Berna's parents in Cork and made himself known. They wish to see me before agreeing to the marriage. Berna wants a big wedding. How can I be happy for this when the sun is going down so quickly in front of me? The power of the bush is closing in and for the first time in years I feel fear.

I get up and turn my back on the river. Kango is standing with the last light on his black skin. He must have followed me. My .375 is in my right hand as I walk towards him and my feet are heavy on the loose sand. I climb up the bank towards the Chev pointing its metal grill at the river.

"I'm going, Kango."

"I know. They have been saying this for two days in the valley."

"I'm sorry but you know why. This will all change. It won't be good for us as it was before. You join the new hunter and make yourself rich. That's all there seems to be. I have left money for you now."

"When do you go, baas?"

"Now. I'm going now."

I get into the Chevrolet Impala and stab the starter. Obediently the engine turns. I switch on the lights, put the car into gear, check that the tank is full and begin the journey. I won't use his language again, and eventually I shall forget all his words.

∼

## DEAR READER

∽

Reviews are the most powerful tools in our kitty when it comes to getting attention for Peter's books. This is where you can come in, as by providing an honest review you will help bring them to the attention of other readers.

If you enjoyed reading *The Big River,* and have five minutes to spare, we would really appreciate a review (it can be as short as you like). Your help in spreading the word and keeping Peter's work alive is gratefully received.

Please post your review on the retailer site where you purchased this book.

Thank you so much.
Heather Stretch (Peter's daughter)

PS. We look forward to you joining Peter's growing band of avid readers.

# ACKNOWLEDGEMENTS

∼

Our grateful thanks go to our *VIP First Readers* for reading *The Big River* prior to its official launch date. They have been fabulous in picking up errors and typos helping us to ensure that your own reading experience of *The Big River* has been the best possible. Their time and commitment is particularly appreciated.

Agnes Mihalyfy (United Kingdom)
Daphne Rieck (Australia)
Hilary Jenkins (South Africa)
Mike Carter (United Kingdom)
Nolan Kee (United Kingdom)

Thank you.
　　Kamba Publishing

Manufactured by Amazon.ca
Acheson, AB